Bert Random crawled int
over a decade later with
dusty trainers, and a chao.
has taken him until now tc
begin piecing it all together.
a variety of online and print   ~pannered is
his first book.

Reviews for **Spannered**:

Its evocative descriptions will echo with anybody who has been to free parties anywhere or anytime, then or since. It's all there – the highs, the lows, the intense friendships, the casualties, the transformation of some derelict zone into a temporary playground. Writing about music without lyrics is notoriously difficult, but the author has a real sense of the physical impact of a snare, a kick drum or a blast of 303 on the bodies of dancers... This book is bang on.
'Transpontine' (history-is-made-at-night.blogspot.com)

Finally it's here, a vivid and lucid account of the urban squat party experience from the inside... this is the real deal.
Chris Liberator (Stay Up Forever Records)

I've been waiting ages for someone to write an account of the free party scene in the UK in the 90's... Spannered covers just one night at a Bristol warehouse party, but it's a long and eventful one. This is an intense and accurate portrayal of the free party scene and contains some of the best depictions of raves that I've ever read.
'Free Party Person' (freepartypeople.wordpress.com)

Love it! A really fun read, with some great visual descriptions of the weirdest moments.
DAVE the Drummer (Hydraulix Records)

SPANNERED

Bert Random

**ƳSPANNERED
ĻBOOKS**

Published in paperback 2011 by Spannered Books
Reprinted 2012
www.spanneredbooks.com
in association with SilverWood Books, Bristol, BS1 4HJ
www.silverwoodbooks.co.uk

Second Edition

Text copyright © Bert Random 2011
All artists retain the copyright to their respective works
Tracklist design by Sara

The right of Bert Random to be identified as the author of this work
has been asserted by him in accordance with the Copyright,
Designs and Patents Act 1988.

All rights reserved. No part of this publication may be reproduced,
stored in a retrieval system, or transmitted in any form or by any means,
electronic, mechanical, photocopying, recording or otherwise,
without prior permission of the copyright holder.

ISBN 978-1-906236-57-1

British Library Cataloguing in Publication Data
A CIP catalogue record for this book is available from the British Library

Set in Palatino by SilverWood Books
Printed in England on paper certified as being from responsible sources

In memory of
Stevie, Dorian, Jay,
Emily, Candace, Abi,
Lez, Caz, and Glove

For S and F – the best rush yet

Dedicated to all the Free Party
Crew – 'aving it in a field somewhere!

"So now, less than five years later, you can go up on a steep hill in Las Vegas and look West, and with the right kind of eyes you can almost see the high-water mark – that place where the wave finally broke and rolled back."

HUNTER S. THOMPSON – *Fear and Loathing in Las Vegas*

"It is a bit embarrassing to have been concerned with the human problem all one's life and find at the end that one has no more to offer by way of advice than 'Try to be a little kinder'."

ALDOUS HUXLEY

01 / Joey Beltram – Energy Flash

We hear music.

It's some distance away but it's definitely there. A steady rhythmic thud drifts over the rooftops, drawing us towards it. Chumpee's eyes are gleaming with mischief in the moonlight and we both start to go a little bit faster, unconsciously walking in time with the distant drum pattern. I hand him a spliff as two cars stuffed full of partyheads crawl past, while we cross a bridge above an inner-city motorway and continue on to a dejected part of town. Roofless warehouses line the opposite bank of the canal, stars visible in the dark blue sky through the broken windows.

I look back and see the straggling line of people who have come with us from our house in St Nicks to this no-mans land between a river and a drive-through. There are at least twenty of us, maybe thirty in all: Gonzo, Goon, Little My, Caspar, Helen, Acid Bob, Zak, Corrine, Dreads Dave, Harry, the Graces, Abdi, Ramona, loads more. People from all over the country and all over the world, who have landed in Bristol and been unable to leave. Survivors from the convoys; European techno-freaks who would follow a beat anywhere; Americans who spent their teens following the Grateful Dead; crazy Canadians on maxed-out credit cards. A proper bunch of randoms.

Most of us haven't known each other long – a few months, a few years, a handful of longer friendships – but something has just clicked during nights and days on the dancefloor. We are tight.

Chumpee laughs to himself at nothing in particular, just happy to be out and about, feeling the concrete of his recently adopted city beneath his feet. More cars bounce past us, tunes blaring, friends and strangers shouting 'hellos' as they go by. They all take the next right, just up ahead, underneath a massive fly-over with its constant rumble of traffic.

"Here we go then," shouts Chumpee.

We follow the steady stream of cars into the abandoned corner of a disused trading estate that's holding its breath, waiting to be demolished. The music is louder now; we're nearly there. I can feel butterflies trying to take off in my stomach, a rush of adrenaline and excitement shivering through my body. It's beginning to get crowded; there are badly parked cars everywhere along this dead-end street, people spilling out of them into the cold night air, their breath like dragons', drifting away. The anticipation is palpable. It's tickling my neck. You can feel the electricity as people congregate.

A wire fence surrounds a jumble of large crumbling buildings, a bottleneck has developed around the mesh double gate. Eventually I glide through with Chumpee, Gonzo and Little My, as the group of us that walked here together is slowly absorbed into the greater mass. We will regroup in various forms throughout the night.

There are fucking *loads* of people here; at times it seems everyone I have ever known and more. We can't walk further than a few feet without having to stop and hug someone hello; it takes us ages to get across the carpark. Half the pub's here, all having heard the same rumour, seen the same handful of flyers. So are people I partied with back in 1990. And someone I met once at a festival four years ago and haven't seen since. People I've worked with at various times, with varying degrees of success.

There are old skaters from Dean Lane, a handful of exes, and even one or two people that I went to school with. Old '92 ravers out of retirement, house divas in fake fur, indie kids and students, travellers, punks, and dreads. All laughing and chatting, stamping their feet in the chill of the clear May night, wondering if this is really going to happen. Nervous and drunk and speeding and straight and stoned and rushing and tripping in equal measure.

Double doors loom before us, and inside the warehouse we can see a fire burning, cold party crew huddled around it. Hordes of people are flooding into the derelict building, looking around in expectation. The music that we heard on our way up the street seems to have been coming from some monster car stereo which is thumping away just outside the gate – it's noisy inside the warehouse, but only with the hum of human chatter, and the clatter and crashing of people doing *stuff*. A yellow Bedford truck is parked with its backdoors open; a human chain is taking bits of kit from the van and disappearing into the darkness at the far end of the building – racks of amps, boxes full of wiring, the precious decks, speakers and finally the bassbins that take small gangs of people to carry. Everything we need is arriving because we've reached critical mass, we've got enough people here to get the soundsystem in and set up without the police coming and grabbing the lot. Too many of us for it to be worth their while kicking up a fuss. Safety in numbers.

We do a few deals as we wander around – sell a bit of weed, sort out some pills. I buy myself a few trips off of Old Owen, an indestructible sixties hippie who just refuses to slow down. In the early hours he can often be seen staggering and mumbling to himself, furtling in his many layers of clothes looking for another dose of his random drug of choice this week. Caspar sees me sorting myself out, trying not to drop the acid in the dark, making sure I know what stuff is in which pocket. (Fags, weed and solids, acids, rizlas, roach, lighter, cash. Front door key on a string round my neck. Everything where it should be.)

"What you got there?" he asks in his distinctive European accent, his teeth grinding through the speed.

"Acids," I say. "Screaming Buddhas. Meant to be good ones. Want to split one?"

"Go'wan then," he smiles. "Can you get any more? I want to get properly focked up."

"Of course."

I split one of the thick cardboard tabs with him, feeling that psychosomatic tingle as I swallow my half. Immediately I feel a little bit high. I lead Caspar to Old Owen, and leave them chatting. As I walk away Cas buys another couple of tabs, and chucks them straight down his neck. It's the last I'll see of him for a while.

My eyes slowly become accustomed to the shapes forming from the shadows as I wander, skinning up in my hand, getting a sense of the space. There's shit everywhere, huge piles of bricks, pallets, debris from whatever this building was before it was left to rot. Most of it has been pushed into great mounds against the walls, but there is still plenty of crap on the floor to stumble over. The huge room is split by a line of columns holding up the corrugated roof. An exposed metal framework stretches across the ceiling and bare breezeblock walls stretch for a hundred-and-fifty metres or so in one direction, about half that wide. Two head-high black slabs of speaker stack frame the decks at the far end. They loom silently over the space; currently a dead space, a nothing space, a space waiting to be changed. The activity behind the decks is frantic now, with wires and dreadlocks snaking everywhere in the half darkness. A few snatches of music burst through the system, screeching in from nowhere at such a volume that I jump and nearly spill the weed. Testing, testing, one, two, three. Not long now.

I look for a friendly face to share the spliff. In the half-light just inside the warehouse doors there's the silhouette of a bloke with a huge bunch of balloons. He's got a canister of gas next to him and a little production line going. The balloons are given to people passing by, or have flowers tied to the bottom of their string and are left to float almost forgotten above the crowd. Helen and Norm, who's been dragged out to his first party at the age of forty-six, are having a lovely time, pissed up, inhaling helium and squeaking, 'I love you' at each other. The Balloon man grins to himself and just keeps on filling balloons.

Gonzo is standing five feet away, laughing at the squeaking, so I pass him the spliff and we wander round the fire, talking about who we've seen, giggling at the absurdity of this many freaks gathering together in one place.

This is different; this isn't a fifty people in the basement of a squat in St Pauls. This is hundreds, maybe thousands, of people from all over the place. It feels good, like something that's been bubbling away for a while suddenly gained some momentum, suddenly became real again, here, now, around us.

It's tangible.

I can taste it.

02 / Jones & Stephenson –
The First Rebirth

Here comes the noise.

It creeps up on us, quietly at first, attracting people out of the shadows, inviting us to make this derelict space a dancefloor. The volume reaches a gratifyingly loud level and I realise that this is really going to happen, this is really going to go off.

The music has caught the masses. It sounds vaguely like a distant choir, like a snatch of sweet, sharp voices sampled and made strange, and as it flows into its simple rhythm the crowd begins to gather and sway.

Clanks and clicks and cymbals and samples fall into place and give the beat a framework, an invitation to land. Tension grows; *anticipation* grows as everybody waits for the drums. Slowly the overlapping voices converge towards a point, then it happens: a **boom** like the sky splitting, a tight solid sound, hard and fast. The 4/4 kickdrum takes over our lives and sweeps us as one from a sea of nodding heads to a forest of flailing arms. Shouts go up as cymbals crash and snare drums roll.

The beat drops out for a second, there's another frantic snare roll, then it crashes back in, harder and nastier, a fatter sound, a bit flanged at the edges, driving us into a frenzy. Screams and shouts and whistles and yelps pour out, pure enthusiasm for this exact moment in time and space. To stomp and dance here for the rest of our lives feels

like the best idea we've ever had. The bass drives us on as the noises rise and rise towards another point, pulling us all up with them.

The voices abruptly stop, and another vicious snare roll rips through the air, followed by a twisted bastard of a noise. Short, razor-sharp squeals shoot up and up, with the crowd riding this wave of sound. The beat is still our solid base but the noises... oh fuck the noises... They scream around my head and tell me to let go. I have no control. I really start to dance, not thinking, not worrying, just being. This is pure instinct, twisting and turning, shuffling and stomping; my whole body spasming in short sharp shocks, a puppet whose string is jerked to a 4/4 beat. The cacophony of angels comes back in and my head bursts with the rush, the joy, the lift. This is it. This is everything. For this moment nothing else matters, all conscious thought has dropped away... yesterday – tomorrow – the future... fuck that...

NOW.

Now is all we need.

I hear the crowd lose it and open my eyes. The sight that greets them is a fucking delight. The rapid strobe picks out my fellow dancers – Chumpee punching the air, Little My stomping in circles, Nina doing her tying-shoelaces jungle dance slowed to techno pace and looking wicked. Goon, Helen, Gonzo, Ramona, Polly, Dreads Dave, the Graces and everyone. I am surrounded by people I love, all going crazy. We cluster around the speakers and together experience a truly magical moment, the sort that happens only a select few times in a life. The joy is physical as more and more of our crew flow into the middle of the floor. I smile and receive smiles in return. We exhort each other to even greater displays of blatant public happiness, as the tune storms towards another peak, the bleeps squealing up towards oblivion and the voices soaring across the air; with the drums driving it all on, the everlasting bass that commands you to move and the snares getting loudER and loUDER and LOUDER and LOUDER... before suddenly cutting out, leaving us floating on the bare bones of that huge experience. The heavenly voice. The DJ switches off the deck; the record slows and grinds to a halt. We erupt in appreciation for this incredible piece of music.

Everyone is glowing.

I feel inspired – inspired to do some good quality Class A drugs. So after a few floating-on-air hugs, I drift back outside.

03 / Robotman – Do Da Do
(Plastikman Acid House Mix)

I float into the glow of a huge bonfire that has been started in the carpark, old pallets being dragged from all over site to ward off the midnight cold. My vision is jittery from the acid; everything's glowing and each movement in front of me leaves trails of shifting light behind it. There seem to be more angles to the world than when I stepped into that warehouse half an hour ago. From the outside it looks surprisingly full of smoke, but people are already on the case to sort it out. The smouldering ashes inside are being scooped onto a big sheet of plywood, to be added to the main fire outside, and a Welsh punk nutter called Marty is shimmying up a drainpipe to the roof. His red and black striped jumper reaches the top to cheers and heckles from down below, then he rips back a bit of plastic roof, creating a chimney through which the lingering smoke quickly flows. Soon the steam that rises from a few thousand dancing bodies will be thicker than the smoke.

    A sharper kick drum cuts through from inside the warehouse as the DJ starts to test the system, pushing up the volume. Across the carpark huddles of heads start bouncing in perfect time. Feet start to tap, knees start to rock, backsides start to bob. Chatting and scoring and wheeling and dealing are all good fun, but everyone can feel a little dance coming on. The stars are out. It's gonna be a beautiful night.

    Chumpee's standing by the fire now, swaying in time

to the music, chatting with Gonzo. Flicking spliff ash into the flames, shouting hellos and exchanging hugs with half the people who go past, they look as happy as pigs in shit, like this is their real place in the world. A space made just for them.

"Have you seen that?" asks Gonzo after a big cuddle, gesturing over my shoulder. Behind me there is another warehouse, about thirty feet from the one we've colonized for the night. It's joined to our one by a long sloping walkway, covered by a two storey high strip of corrugated metal. Three quarters of the way along this roof is sagging drastically, only held up by a humungous pile of pallets which are half-crushed under the weight. It all looks completely unstable.

"Remind me not to sit under there later," he deadpans.

"Fucking right. I bet someone climbs it," I reply.

In the corner behind us a huddle of blokes in baseball caps start painting and stencilling all over a big light wall, letterforms taking shape in quick fluid movements, the smell of the spray paint drifting over with each hiss.

"Hello lovely," says Chumpee, for a brief moment not dishing out hugs and drugs to passers-by.

"Alright, gorgeous? Got any pills left?" I ask.

He drops a couple into my hand, refusing the offered notes, and hugs me so hard my ribs nearly crack. I give him a big smacker on the lips and he lets me go.

"Thanks geezer." I say, holding one of the pills up to the light, trying to work out the pattern imprinted on one side.

"Doves," he says as I squint, "silver ones. Good 'un's!"

"Deefffinitely good ones," says Gonzo, swaying and grinning slightly, as he focuses on trying to open his next tin of beer, his eyes rolling gently back in their sockets.

"Ha!" I laugh. "Fuck, this is wicked – so many people… And did you see the size of those bassbins?"

"Yep – and more kit arriving all the time," says Chumpee,

pointing to the gate where another massive crusty truck is crawling through the crowds, presumably full of speakers, lights and people.

I can't help myself and start to laugh, bouncing up and down on the balls of my feet. We chit-chat and share a smoke or two, the conversation easy with the familiarity of a year spent sharing a house – a year of good drugs, late nights and midday breakfasts. Someone walks past and sticks UV cardboard spanners to our tops. At some point we drift back into the warehouse, shuffling and chatting, saying hello to hundreds of people, sharing hundreds of smiles. Almost absent-mindedly I neck one of the pills with a swig of water; bitter on my tongue and chunky in my throat, the MDMA sinks through my gullet into my stomach where it is digested within minutes. From there it's quickly in and out of my liver and into my blood stream, travelling at three miles an hour through my thick red veins and capillaries. About thirty-five minutes after I swallow it the active chemical compounds, mostly MDA, hit my brain where they stimulate synapses, causing serotonin to flood, giving me a widescreen, surround-sound increase in the sensation I process, an increase in the strength of my feelings, a gleaming sense of well-being…

CLICK! A chemical trigger goes off inside my head and fires my consciousness hurtling around my skull. A rush grips my whole body and my mind synapse-surfs like a bullet spiralling through the grooves in a gun barrel. It's a feeling so complex it's beyond description, yet as simple as ABC. Sharp but fluffy, clear yet fuzzy, simultaneously deeply personal and widely communal. My nerve endings feel like they are expanding, stretching out beyond my body, my sense of touch escalating out of all proportion. Someone squeezes my hand as they walk past; I don't see who it is but for an instant I am transported by the smooth firm hand that touches mine. The sheer joy of the briefest contact overwhelms me. My mind focuses on my hand; I consider it in some detail. I don't look at it, because my eyes are still closed…

I feeeeeeeeeeeeeeeeeeeeeeeeeeeeeeeeeeel it.

I feel the microscopic trace of residual warmth that my squeezer has left behind, almost dissipated already, its energy lost from me and returned to the universe.

I feel the tiniest indentations of the skin and sinew of my hand.

I feel the blood pumping, filling my veins.

Booming through my body.

Booming through me.

Booming through.

Booming.

Boom boom

I emerge from the maze inside my mind and focus on the music. The physical manifestation of the sound vibrates my internal organs and stomps up my spine, meeting the abstract, cognitive experience of the tune in what is left of my brain. My legs are beginning to feel peculiar. I wobble, giggle, stagger and gently bump the person next to me. We both apologize at the same time, start laughing at the same time and both start to dance again at the same time. Ha. Wicked.

The MDMA insinuates itself into my system and my eyes start to jitter. I feel them roll back in my head, as my eyelids close for a moment with another rush. My jaw tightens, and my body rides the huge crashing waves. With each breaker there is simply more of me, more brain processes, more feelings, more sensations. When I open my eyes again focusing isn't actually difficult but it is very different. Like looking through a tilt shift lens, whatever I focus on is clear and crisp, to the exclusion of everything else around it. The longer I centre on something the more... the more... the more *real* that particular object begins to feel. The focus at the edges of my vision is fuzzy but the centre of my gaze is clearer than ever. The longer I stare at the bassbin, the more its intrinsic bassbin-ness becomes clear to me, the deeper I sink into its atomic structure, the more I know the bassbin, understand the bassbin.

Love the bassbin.

But the second I look away, the second my eyes slide onto something else, the glow of the bassbin fades and whatever I happen to look at next becomes the most real, most solid, most defined thing in my universe. Everything else around the new subject of my gaze fades into insignificance. This is why falling in love on ecstasy is so hard to avoid, and sometimes not a great idea.

Through all these thoughts I have been dancing. Slowly and smoothly, I think. Sometimes to every other beat, other times just swaying gently, only hitting the sixteenth or thirty-second beat. My movements are guided by the rise

and the fall of the rush in my head, the waves of sensation that hit my body, the waves of intense physical pleasure that repeatedly wash through me. The DJ is playing some hard but high tunes; chunky house, merging into old acid, the occasional Belgian hardcore hoover classic slipping in nicely with bubbling German trance. Simple drum patterns take on a funk of their own with the benefit of repetition, the loop inviting us in, asking us to get comfortable, enticing us to learn the rhythm and catch the break. I find myself dancing with a big crew; Chumpee, Gonzo, Ramona, Zak, Polly, most of people who walked here with us, and loads of other friends, old and new. Near the back of the dancefloor we have space to skip about, chase each other, pull faces, and play silly buggers. It's smiles and hugs all round; spliffs and pipes, water and booze, pills and wraps are all shared with gladness. What a night to be alive. We dance through the crowd to get closer to the speakers, about ten of us holding onto Chumpee's four foot long dreadlocks so we don't get separated in the heaving crowd.

A simple four-beat bass loop comes to the fore in the mix, a scattered drum pattern skittering along behind it. Out of this simplicity an acid line rises; the sound of the Roland TB 303. That signature noise takes over, unlike anything else in the world, an alien sound, a machine melody, a strange noise from another star. Constantly changing, drawing us with it, edging up and down in the tiniest of increments. Occasional pauses in either beat or bass gives the tune a structure, but the sweet squelch just keeps going, never quite dropping out, for so long never quite peaking. We are all far gone and out now, there is nothing happening but dancing; no other focus, no deals being done, no shouted conversations. Just the movement. Eyes half-shut, we sense each other as we swell and shift through the larger crowd around us, all the time the acidline pulling us up, making us higher and higher and higher. It just keeps on going, always refining, bubbling, mutating; it feels like I have been dancing to this record for years, for my whole life, for my whole glorious life. The beat drops completely and the acid hits a holding pattern, an intricate mobius loop. A synth string section sweeps from the speakers and tickles the back of my neck, giving me goosebumps. Literally, the hairs on my arms and the nape of my neck rise. I don't remember ever feeling this good before. I look around me and I can see that they all feel it too. Without the beat to drive our feet we just stand and vibrate and raise our hands. The acid jumps up; one notch, then two, then three, four and five in quick succession, peaking just as the beat drops back in…

We are taken as one to a better place.

Another tune starts to mix in, snares rolling over and over each other; the beautiful, perfect, acidline finally fades away to nothing. Zak looks at me as I shake my head, all of us doing the same, like waking from a trance, arriving after a long journey. He starts giggling hysterically, tears rolling down his cheeks; he hangs from Chumpee's shoulder shaking with laughter. It's contagious. Hugs are exchanged as we all laugh too. He knows we all just shared a moment, all just felt *something*. Something *big*. A sense of something *bigger* than ourselves; a sense of the universe, of gods, of the vast spaces within each of the atoms inside each of us, of our own improbability, of the infinite possibilities contained in all the things we don't know we don't know. Whatever you want to call it, he's right. We did feel something.
    We felt a sense of *belonging*.
    Felt good.

The housey tunes grind to a halt inside the building; there is a second of silence, with its brief background buzz of dazed and confused conversation, before a bassdrum sounds like a thunderclap and something harder and spacier begins. Bassline squelches build up and up, and then burst into life; a huge acidic churning sound revolves around in the damp air, echoing, phasing, a noise like the tectonic plates of an alien world grinding against each other. The lights flash through the darkness, illuminating the rising steam. Fine drops of rain are drifting in through the hole in the roof, freeze-framing in the strobe. I stop for a second and let it fall on me, but it's only a pause. Really, I just want to move deeper into the crowd. I follow my crew and forge right down the front, towards the speakers, the amps, the DJs, the noise.

Towards the source.

04 / Hardfloor – Aceperience

"Alright then bloke," cries a West Country accent; all warm, rolling rrrrr's and a different way with vowels. Arms grab me from behind, from out of the darkness. It's Goon – one of a kind, out of his mind, having a wicked time. Fuelled by scrumpy, speed and pills, he's one of the greatest dancers in the world. Sloppy and ragged, he shakes around me, ecstasy taking out all of his rough edges, turning him into Mr Soft at a thousand miles per hour. Chumpee and me just found him one night, literally just found him, sitting on a wall outside the club all of us had just left. Earlier in the night we'd both noticed and commented admiringly on this mad dancing bloke, all flappy arms and slinky legs, storming round the place, one minute in front of the speaker, the next stomping along the balcony, then at the front of the stage giving it loads. Wondering what he was doing, sitting steaming and smoking in the cold air, we'd gone over and said hello. He'd blagged a train to get here, just for the club, and had nowhere to stay. He was planning to go and sleep in the train station, but we made him come back to St Nicks with us instead, for a night of more pills, cider and hot knives.

Talking to him was easily one of the best decisions we ever made.

He gives me a huge cuddle, and I willingly disappear into his gangly frame, but I politely decline the dubious looking plastic bottle he waves in my face.

"Ow're you," he asks.

"Rahhh! Wicked!" is all I can say, my head spinning with the drugs and the dancing. Conversation is momentarily impossible and, thankfully, unnecessary. One look into Goon's far-away eyes, so full of life, so proud to be alive, to be here, to be dancing – one look tells you all, leaves you sure. He says, "YYEESS!" with all his heart and mind, with all his limbs; he's gives all he has to give, then goes and finds more. What a fucking STAR. The all important eye contact is made through the half darkness, and we dance around each other, copying each others stupid movements and silly faces, skipping like Morecombe and Wise one moment, spinning like tops the next. A huge buildup washes over us from the dancefloor – strange sounds and piercing snares, building up and up, seizing the whole building in its grasp. We stare at each other as the pitch of the stabbing synth-noise gets higher and higher and the snare-roll gets faster and faster... And then we dance like demons when everything comes crashing back in – bassdrum, acidlines, screaming voices, everything. A glorious noise. The place explodes, shouting, whooping, and hollering. In the distance we can hear Chumpee shouting, "G'WAN MOOVE YER BODEEEE".

We dance, doing the 'Goon' – punching the air in huge floppy circles with one hand, happy as fuck. In the darkness of the early hours people's drugs and the DJ's music peak in perfect symmetry. It's not the last time we will hear that tune tonight.

"D'you wanna walk to the 24-hour garage with me, I'm gonna go now before I get too fucked, innit!" he shouts over the music a few minutes later, as the sound of waves crashing onto a beach and a blue-sky acid line circles around us. I gaze at him, standing there looking as fucked as is humanly possible without needing constant kidney dialysis.

"Yeah, why not," I shout. "A little walk will probably do me good, and I need some more fags."

"Follow me," he shouts, smiling, "I'll be right behind you!"

We leave the building with a short list of requests for drinks, rizlas and 'baccy. We promise to do our best to remember everything, and fall out into the real world. A world we want very little to do with. Two policemen wander down the road ahead of us, noting a few car registrations as they go. We go into innocent mode, trying to walk in a fairly straight line and everything, avoiding eye contact as if out lives depend upon it.

"Just look straight ahead," I mutter. "Please don't try to make friends with them, Goon."

He grins. "'Course not. Would I?"

Past them (looking straight ahead), past their cars with a few more sat talking into radios (still looking straight ahead), and we finally feel a little bit more relaxed. I realise I've been holding my breath. I also realise that all my drugs are just in my pocket, ready to be busted. Once we're round the corner I fish them out and stuff them down one of my socks, in case we get pulled on our way back. Fucking idiot.

"There's no way they can stop it now," I say out loud, hoping for agreement from the eternal optimist Goon.

"No way," he laughs. "I'd like to see 'em try, too many people, definitely too many people."

As we walk and talk a steady flow of stuffed cars crawl past us, heads hanging out of windows, following the thud-thud-thud-thud. One car stands out – the back tires are bulging with the weight it's carrying and every time it goes over a bump the exhaust scrapes the floor. It's Mad Billie's car, crammed full of drooling speedfreaks and spun-out ket-heads; there are at least five people squeezed onto the back seat and another two or three in the boot, from the faces we can see squashed up against the windows of the tiny two door hatchback. Billie salutes, grinning, as he drives past.

"Did you go to that party on Steart beach two weeks ago?" I ask Goon.

"Oh yes, whatta messy night," he says. "I can't remember fuck all about it. Where were you, were you there?" He waves his bottle of scrumpy as he talks.

"Nah, was on the door at Trinity, and then took down the décor when it finished at four," I say. "Me and Silver Grace were going to come out afterwards, but got kind of stuck at hers."

"Mate, you missed a good party, I think. It was reallllllly weird. Has anyone told you about the camels?"

"Yes, someone did mention camels!" I laugh, "Frankie I think. I assumed it was just a random Frankie hallucination. Camels? Really?"

"It was fucked up. We were in the middle of the long stretch of beach, with Hinckley Point glowing across the water. Bloody nothing for miles in any direction. Bob went off..."

"Acid Bob, Hairy Bob or Lord Bob?"

"Acid Bob. He went to get firewood in the middle of the night, was gone for hours and then came back with a tiny selection of twigs. Like four or five twigs. None of 'em bigger than a finger! And he was so proud of finding 'em too."

I smile at his heartfelt love for Acid Bob, one of his dedicated partners in crime.

"Anyway, like I said, nothin' for miles. Then a car turns up in the morning, towing a massive trailer thing, a horse box. I'm sat there with Bob, Gollum and that, all squinting trying to see what is getting out of the trailer when someone shouts, 'They're camels!' We all went, 'Yeah right, fuck off' but then they got a bit closer..." I try to interrupt with a question, but can't get it past my giggling. "... and there they were – three camels, humps an' all, walking across the pebbles, like the fucking Arabian Nights. Camels walking around with that dirty big power station in the background. Did my bloody head in."

"Did anyone go and talk to the owner?"

"Nah, every one was so freaked out we just stared 'til they got back into their trailer and buggered off. God knows what the bloke thought of us, loads of shit-faced munters and two soundsystems banging away at eleven o'clock on a Sunday morning."

We arrive at the 24-hour garage, its forecourt full of cars full of party people. We join the queue and try to remember what we came to get, randomly shouting words at each other until we think we've got the list. The whole queue bobs in time to the loudest car stereo on the forecourt, while we watch the guy behind the night time safety screen. This is an utter nightmare for him; it's usually a boring, easy shift, but now these weird-looking creatures keep arriving, and they've got him running all over the shop. Some of them are climbing on the newspaper stand and the barbeque coal to get a better look inside the locked garage, pressing their hairy faces and bald heads against the glass trying the check out the chocolate isle and the cigarettes. He rushes around throwing the rizlas, chewing gum, fags and Lucozade I get for me and Goon through the hole in his screen, anxious to get the freaks off his forecourt as soon as possible. When he tells us how much it all costs I see musical notes and washes of colour float from his mouth. We give the harassed face through the glass a beaming, pilled-up smile as we pay and the glare we get in return almost shatters the glass.

"You doing Glastonbury this year?" Goon asks me.

"Yeah. I'm gonna have to jump the fence though, unless I can get some work."

"Hrrrm, yeah, me too," he says.

"Tom says he'll drive a van-full of people down there for a fiver each, then come back and do a pick-up on the Monday," I say.

"I love a plan, me, and that's a good 'un," says Goon, "Just hope the getting in goes better than last year."

"Why, did you get caught?"

"Bloody hell geezer, getting in was a nightmare last year. Haven't I told you this before? I was the tallest of my lot, so I was given a leggie up and pulled myself onto the wall. The first place we tried was disastrous. I managed to drag myself up, and looked over the wall, and I was staring straight at a policeman. In the police compound. You sure I haven't told you this before?"

"No way have you told me this before," I say.

"Maaaaaate," he grins, "it bloody gets worse. So I drops back down and we run like fuck to get away. Next place we tried, I got up onto the wall alright and lifted one bloke over then a couple of bags then a few more people. I pull up this big, fat, pissed bastard, who wobbles and fucks down the other side, straight on to my rucksack."

"Oh, shiiiiit," I say. "Anything broken?"

"Not on him, he just got up and wandered off, shitfaced."

"Thank fuck for that."

"He was fine. He'd fucking cracked the plastic on me two flagons of scrumpy in my backpack though."

"Nnnnoooooooooo…"

"I didn't even realise 'til I'd been carrying it for twenty minutes. I felt something running down the back of my trousers n'thought I'd shat meself or something. Everything I had was wet and sticky, spare keks, socks, fags, fucking everything."

"Mate. What a 'mare."

"Tell me about it. I still had a wicked time but I'd like to do it in trousers that aren't dunked in cider this year. For one thing it will make it easier to persuade people to let me sleep in their tents. I'm gonna travel light, two flagons of cider and the clothes I'm standing in, and that's it! And no helping anyone!"

I'm laughing again by now.

He lowers his voice to a comedy-whisper, which is still loud as fuck. He can't talk any other way, 'Deaf in one ear, see' as he likes to remind us when we shush him because he's slaughtered and shouting. "There's a girl at the warehouse who was at that party on the beach. Had a little dance with her earlier. She's, she's... hrrrmmmm."

He tries to articulate it, but then just raises his eyebrows and gurns a bit to explain just how '...' she is.

"Oh yeah? Is it time for the Goon charm? Careful now."

"Yeah, well, at Steart she kept on jumping on me all night. Loads of little dances and cuddles. Just kept turning up next to me. Now I'm shit at noticing that stuff, and even I noticed it. So I says to her, 'You won't want to know me when the sun comes up.'"

"And?"

"She didn't want to know me when the sun came up."

"Aawww! That's very mean."

"I could see her point I wasn't really at my most suave and sophisticated."

"Why? You're a gent when you want to be," I say.

"Hhrrmm. I'm pretty sure I went for a paddle with my shoes and socks still on at some point. Rolled me trousers up to me knees though. Not a good look..."

We're almost back at the warehouse. The police have fucked off, and the space where they were parked has been filled. There are loads of people, fucking *loads* of them, all with one thing on their minds; getting into that warehouse and fucking having it.

"Do you want to split a pill?" I ask, knowing the answer as I ask the question.

"Ooooo, go'wan then. Do you want a little bomb of MDMA?"

"Sounds like a good deal to me."

We stop before entering the warehouse's double doors and exchange drugs and hugs. "You're a fucking star," I say as we crush each other. He returns the squeeze and we re-enter the glowing building, refreshed from our walk. We have the supplies we need and fresh drugs gently lowering themselves into our brains and bodies.

Let's go.

05 / Pump Panel – Ego Acid

Fucking hell.

The building is full. Full of people, full of light, full of sound. The dingy, dark, half-empty warehouse we left thirty minutes ago has transformed. There are blinding strobes and colours flashing through the air. Huge inflatable stars hang from the rafters, forming a soft white ceiling above the clouds of steam that rise from hot, wet bodies. Intricate psychedelic backdrops cover every wall and a huge screen attached to a scaffold tower has multicoloured, mind-bending visuals projected onto it, always changing, flowing and mutating. There are dancers in UV costumes scattered through the crowd, giving it loads.

Best of all, the music is twice as loud as before. More speakers have been added, I can see them at the front, towering over the crowd, pouring harsh fast acid tunes into the damp air. Our favourite kind of music; drums and bass hammering away, unreal sounds oscillating wildly as the DJ brings in the next record. A noise like a jet plane taking off swirls up and out of the speakers, twisting around the room, twisting up my head. I can't resist it, I plunge headlong into the crowd, absorbing it all, enjoying it all. Goon is next to me fucking havin' it, whirling around as the sharp, smooth, sound rises again taking us all up with it. A different 303 pattern takes over, becomes the most important thing in the world, repeating and looping over a deep synth noise rumbling away in the background.

The extra loud bass-heavy kickdrum from the next slab of vinyl coming in is instantly noticeable as it crunches down bang on time. A particular squelch escapes from the churn, getting more and more frantic, soaring higher and higher, before it and everything else cuts dead.

Silence. Just for a second. A plummy male voice cries out from the speakers:

"ExTRAORDINARY!"

And then *everything* comes booming back in around us. A solid wall of noise. Focussed. Dense. We're helpless. There's nothing we can do.

Don't fight it, feel it.

A girl with a golden smile grins in my direction as she spasms around in front of me. Her costume is a jungle of UV netting; yellow, pink, orange and green, like a grass skirt around her waist, wrapped around her chest, topped by a huge headdress attached to her short dreads. She sprays colour around herself, surrounded by insane tracers, this kaleidoscopic halo cascading down her back. The DJ mixes in a classic tune, a whirlwind of sound swirls up and up and up and up and up and up and up and up… before the bass drum stutters and rolls, ending with a pop that launches a sharp, fast wobble of chemically-treated guitar riff. The building shakes with stomping feet and the twisted woman in front of me goes mad; her movements are so sharp, so fast. She is so totally and utterly and effortlessly *there* that I am blown away. Complex movements of her feet flash around at double-time, twice as fast as everyone else, two moves to every beat. Her arms writhe around her body as she stomps on her spot, spraying out as her shuffle widens; still so sharp, right on the beat, her hands rising and falling with the unbearable acid noise. We point at each other through the haze of dust, sweat, smoke and drugs and go for it, showing off to each other, pushing each other on, winding each other up, laughing all the time, getting faster and faster, more and more intricate. Her grin is matched by mine as we dance circles around each other, forming a physical relationship before we even touch. There's a break in the drums and we just stand and quiver, our eyes still locked in. We just shake as the snares grow then the tune kicks again and we're gone. She's lost it now. Her head is shaking from side to side as if she's trying to force her brain out of one ear; her limbs have become a blur, as has her multi-textured dream-costume. Wrapped in her aura of colour this woman is incredible, invulnerable, invincible.

We dance closer to each other, face to face, eye to eye; we imitate each other, arm for arm, stomp for stomp. We stop dancing as the tune begins to fade. We are almost touching. I am almost shaking; from the dancing, the drugs, the people, this person. We smile and have a huge hug; her strong arms squeeze me, making me melt.

"I'm Rez," she says, in a thick Scottish accent.

"I'm Bert," I reply.

She laughs and gives me one last squeeze as we spin away from each other, new found friends. She points towards the soundsystem, smiles and raises an eyebrow – I grin in agreement as she attaches an intricately painted wooden peg, covered in tiny UV swirls and stars, to the sleeve of my t-shirt.

We forge towards the impressive speakers, determined to get as close as possible, determined for it to be as loud as possible. We want to drown in music, we want to submerge ourselves in sound; we want to breathe in the beats, absorb the acid, bounce off the basslines, scream, shout, stomp... yes! We shimmy through the crowd, with me rolling a quick spliff as we go. The first pile of baccy and pot gets bumped out of my hand by a spinning dancer, but I manage to scoop the second lot into a rizla. A quick lick, a scrap of cardboard mashed into one end, kind of, and I've got something that burns, even if it looks like it might fall apart if it doesn't get smoked quickly enough.

Down the front, it's bright and loud and sweaty and fantastic. Goon, Little My and the full crew have all been drawn to the front right speaker, pulled towards the massive rig. There are smiles and hugs, shouted hellos and half-heard replies. It's so fucking loud I can feel my hair moving.

There's a pair of scuffed, dusty trainers poking out of the bottom of one of the bassbins, the twitching body of a reveller curled in a foetal position inside, soaked in low frequencies. I lean forward to check they are alright, but a smile and shake of the head from a nearby dancer stops me.

"It's ok," she shouts, "He's mine, he's alright! Just needs a minute on his own!" She smiles at the muntiness of her fella, and glides in a circle, nudging him with her foot every now and again to get him to raise his head and give her a weak gurning smile. Around him the dance continues. You can feel the love in the room. I pass her the spliff and immediately roll another – easier now I'm not stomping through the crowd at the same time.

Behind the decks a gaggle of people laugh and bob around their DJ – a bloke me and Chumpee call DJ Death, our favourite on the scene. He repeatedly pulls the next record back while fiddling with the pitch control; hoodie up, dark rings under his eyes, generally pale and drawn, his black-pit pupils focussed on the decks and mixer, getting the tempo just right before banging the cross-fader to the middle, smashing the new drum pattern over the top of the tune that is now fading out. He smiles at the ecstatic reaction of the crowd in front of him then quickly turns to his record box, his eyes narrowing in thought –"Now then. What next?"

Someone passes me half a pill and I neck it, someone

passes me a fat spliff and I smoke it, someone passes me a pipe and I fill it. We all smoke it. The music throbs from the speakers, rattling my rib cage. Dancing here, two feet away from thousands of watts of sound it is SO FUCKING LOUD; I can feel the air *inside* my lungs being punched back with every bass-heavy beat. The sweeping strings, the mutating, pulsing trebles, the rounded, bouncy bass all envelop me as if I was actually in the speaker curled up with that bloke. They physically affect me, they desegregate me, they take me and remake me.

The rush starts at my toes and tumbles up my body, travelling so fast it jumps and overtakes itself, racing the sound from the rig that hits me at seven-hundred-and-sixty miles per hour. It reaches my brain, leaving a glowing trail through my nervous system, and makes the hair on the back of my neck stand up, my jaw clench and my eyes roll back in my head. My whole skull rolls over with it, and I trip over my own feet. Then the light bursts out of the top of my head, pulling me back upright, lifting my feet from the floor. I suddenly find I am dancing on air. Smiles are the last things I see around me as I let my eyes shut.

I'm there.

I feel a link with something primeval, not just with my immediate environment, not just with the shit-hot party going on around me. A link with something deeper than that. I feel a connection to my own history of dancing; being a kid shaking to the Beatles and the Stones, a little later to Aretha and Ray; sliding around the kitchen floor as a teenager trying to be as lithe as Prince; bouncing to

Public Enemy and pogoing to the Clash in the skate park on glorious, sunny weekends; walking past Tony's Records on Park Street and being drawn into my first proper record shop by the booming bassline of Smith & Mighty's version of *Walk On By*. I remember being on the verge of adulthood and going to a new squat that friends had just established, and finding it was the crumbling four storey house my dad had lived in until I was eleven. I remember dropping acid in my old part-time bedroom, and sticking my head into the gap between the floorboards and the wall, where the house was falling away from the rest of the terrace into the abandoned graveyard next door. I remember going downstairs to dance to acid house and New Order, watching the ghosts of my childhood dance with me. All of these memories jumble through my mind in seconds. I live them all simultaneously, in a quantum state, bouncing through time and space, everywhere all at once.

I remember the cellars of city centre pubs in 1990 – the steam rising from the vents to the street so thick and fast that passers-by think it's on fire. I remember '91, living in a flat above Bristol's best house DJ – a woman called Ruby who took me under her wing; I remember helping out at the parties she put on with her transvestite co-promoter in little blues clubs and community centres, full of happy, shiny people from all over.

Dancing, dancing, all the time, dancing.

Then, in '92, the big one. Castlemorton. Sitting on a hill, with my back to twenty-five thousand ravers, travellers and weekenders, watching patchwork fields squirm and wriggle one over the other for as far as my munted eyes could see. Circus Warp and the Spirals twisting up my head, the DiY tent glowing in the darkness and saving my life. Onto 1993, a loss of momentum – pay-parties, Universe and all that. Good but not quite right. Moments of brilliance, moments of bleakness.

I remember the handful of friends who died along the way.

Finally, I remember up-to-date dancing; last year, last month, last weekend, Wednesday night, Thursday night, yesterday. A new flush of enthusiasm, new friends arriving in town combining with new sounds, new clubs, new house parties, boat parties, squat parties; every weekend, something happening, somewhere. Stubbornly partying ever harder in the face of looming legislation, specifically being designed to stop all of this and more. All this history leads to here and now. This minute, this second. It trails behind me, but it doesn't weigh me down. It propels me, its momentum. I'm pushed on by everybody I ever danced with, by everybody who has ever danced to garage or house or breaks or hardcore or jungle or trance or techno or acid; I'm possessed by everyone who has ever been moved by music. I feel a link to distant drums of warning and celebration, to the force of rhythm on our cerebral patterns and genetic muscle memories. I remember all this in a split second. Then I am back, here and now, stomping through sound. Still *there*, but *here* as well.

I feel sharp yet loose. My limbs feel nimble, ready to roll. No matter how hectic the music gets my mind seems to anticipate its changes, giving me time to dance, time to move randomly, but to still land something back on the beat, *sharp*, every single time. My lolloping motion disguises a fanatical devotion to the structure of the drums.

A splash of cold water hits my face, cooling and calming; it's a surprise, but a pleasant one. I open my eyes and see Little My and Rez running in amongst the crowd, bright UV plastic water pistols in hand, spraying everyone they know and everyone who looks like they need it. They're playing at being Starsky and Hutch, hiding behind pillars and large people before jumping out and squirting each other. Laughing and dancing all the time they disappear through the crowd, pistols at the ready. Beautiful Corrine is freak-dancing in a big circle, her long straight hair flying around her head, hiding the intense concentration on her face. Tash and Lord Bob have found a ragged old teddy bear and are taking it in turns to waltz it around, lost in a DMT world of their own. Chumpee appears in front of me advancing out of the mass. He's borrowed a long black rubber coat from somewhere and as he approaches me he stretches the front out with both hands and lets it spring back as if he's on a bungee rope. He lets himself fly backwards into the writhing crowd, his Cheshire Cat grin the last thing I see as he beckons me after him. I step forward to follow but pause, as Zak strides past, grinning in the darkness.

"You alright?" I ask the wide-eyed smiler.

"It's been a night of surprises," he replies.

"Such as?"

"How strong this old acid is! Fucking hell…" he laughs.

Before I can ask him who's selling it a mischievous-looking Jude grabs him by the arm and says, "Come on you, I thought we were going to find someone selling booze." His grin gets even bigger as she leads him away. It seems that everyone is having a wonderful time. I laugh as I dive back into the group, following Chumpee's gap-toothed smile towards the rig.

I feel like we could take on the world.

06 / The Infinity Project – Feeling Weird

It's all snapshots from here on in, a series of loosely connected events flashing past me. The one constant is the beat thumping away in the background, the perfect eternal beat. My head seems to be expanding and contracting between heartbeats but I guess that's kind-of normal.

I feel momentarily knackered and really do need to sit down.

Suddenly.

Very.

Light.

Headed.

Ooooooooh.

Wobble.

And breathe.

…

I'm still as high as fuck, but my feet are aching from the total locked-in stomp I have been in for the last… half hour?

Hour?

Two hours?

Fuck knows.

It feels like minutes, but the pre-dawn sky I can see through the hole in the roof tells me it must be a lot later than I think. The continual rushes from the random assortment of pills and powders was something else entirely; it feels like they brushed aside everything I've ever done, started with a clean slate, and re-wrote the world inside my head. I feel porous, open to sensation and suggestion. I've emerged onto a level that seems gentle and light. It takes me a bit by surprise. All of a sudden, for a split second, I don't feel high at all. I feel totally straight. *This* is normal. *This* is how I should feel all the time: relaxed, happy, carefree, my feet bouncing on clouds, my head full of smoke.

The music has changed – the screaming acid turmoil that moved us all so maniacally for the last few hours has been replaced by something mellower. Little bubbles of sound pop around us, around each other, as a voice sample mumbles in the background:

"Forward scanners **on**... prepare for **take-off**."

One particular bubble begins to repeat, bursting on the off-beat, becoming a squeal that becomes one of many; supplying us with the rhythm that is finally completed by the kick drum that bounces in over our heads. It's slower than the last DJ's music but that could be just what is needed. Strings and a choir of voices build-up then fade, passing the baton of upward movement to a high spiralling tone which spins between the speakers before twisting itself inside out and upside down. The beat drops out and the pattern circles down. Another drawled voice sample cuts in:

"A crazy **bulbous punchbag** of soouuunnnnnd   "

Bang on the 'd' a skippy little breakbeat funks its way around the warehouse. People are getting into this now; we are starting to move as one again – the horizon of heads finding a common rhythm, enjoying this change of pace and the space between the beats.

Acid Bob floats past, eyes closed, arms drifting around his body at shoulder height. He's fucking far-out beyond the stars, smiling as he follows his bliss around the dancefloor. He's another wicked dancer; less of a stomper, more of a shuffler, hands in loose fists rocking back and forward in front of his face, grey baggy top slouched around him, shaking as he glides from side to side. His hands fall in front of him, catching an acidline between them, and he grins quietly to himself as he feels the groove roll through his body. He coaxes the sound along, fully focussed on his fingers, seemingly caressing the noise, smiling at it, stroking it, his hands rotating in an ever growing circle around the imaginary universe he cradles, his entire consciousness consumed by the tune. The crowd moves around him as he blindly ebbs and flows through the mass. The dancefloor is rammed with loads of Rez's ultraviolet freak-squad mates, and their weird homemade costumes and full-on ostentatious dancing. Acid Bob floats through everyone, eyes shut, oblivious to everything.

One of the freak-squad has a costume that is darker than the rest. It's formed from moulded plastic pieces, hanging from him like body armour. He looks like a robot designed by HR Geiger. Tiny details and fake circuitry is picked out in UV dots and lines, radiating light against the dark background. Less is more. It helps that he is a wicked dancer. Loose-limbed and funky; he's got a bit of a stomp but always with forward motion, one hand floating by his side, the other in front of him sidewinding though the crowd and guiding his way. I drift behind him for a while, skirting the edge of the writhing horde, just watching him dance. He looks like he's semi-dislocated, like he's going to fall apart any second into a pile of bones, muscle and skin. Dancing near the sides is hazardous; the scree of rubble and pallets and tyres and fuck knows what else slopes down from the walls most of the way along, but he floats through all of it without slowing or missing a beat. Wicked.

Towards the front the crap gets sparser, and here people lean and slump against the breezeblocks. One of the figures pressed to the wall is familiar, a stationary silhouette moving nothing except for one foot that taps completely out of time. It's Caspar. Munted, wankered, helplessly-tripping Caspar.

"Alright mate?" I shout as I swirl past. His pupils are massive black holes, fixed on the inflatables glowing red and orange in the lights above the crowd. He doesn't appear to be blinking very much, though he does have a faint far-away smile on his face. I leave him to it for a bit, dancing around and about with strangers who are soon friends, keeping half a bleary eye on Cas. Arthur is standing nearby with his back to a speaker – shirt off, buff and sweaty; his bald head and short pointed goatee steaming in the glow of the lights. He has a look of ecstasy on his face, and it's obvious why. A beautiful black woman in a scarlet vamp dress is sitting on the speaker stack behind him, and she's tracing lines down his bare back with her long blood-red fingernails. Every time she sweeps the sharp points down to the base of his spine his eyes roll back outrageously. She is utterly blowing his mind and she knows it, grinning out over his head at the crowd, enjoying her total control.

The tunes are fucking banging out of the rig – a skinny bald bloke in a knee-length summer dress is playing some heavy acid, really loud. There are a crowd of other DJs hanging around behind the decks, chatting and drinking

and waiting to snake their way on for play. 'Boys with bags' Ruby calls them, a mostly good-natured, sometimes snidey, ecosystem with politics all of its own. Twenty minutes or so pass before Caspar slowly turns his head towards me. Well, his head turns but his eyes swivel in their sockets to stay fixed on the huge, ever-growing bubble of light floating above the dancefloor. His pupils slowly catch up with the rotation of his head, and he smiles as he tries to focus.

"Beeeeerrrrrrttt!!!" he slurs as we hug. "My friends, my friend… what a night, my, my, my friend, my brother." I laugh and agree, and we dance at each other a bit, smiling.

"Have you been leaning there long – you looked very comfy?" I shout.

"Yes. I think. A long time. A good time, but a long time. I just could *not move*, for so long, but it was still good. The lights…" he trails off.

"More!" he shouts and scans the crowd for Owen, who has managed to find a chair from somewhere, and is sat rocking back and forward next to a speaker. He's got a tiny bit of burnt-out roach clamped in his grinning teeth; every now and again he stands up, puts his hands behind his back and peers round the speaker at the DJ to nod his approval at whatever weird noise has taken his fancy. Then it's back to his chair, leaning and rocking and laughing and pointing and waving his feet about. Utterly shitfaced. Caspar wobbles over to him and shouts a request in his ear. A protracted few moments of fumbling, haggling and struggling to work out money follows, but eventually they do the deal and more lysergic acid diethylamide is ingested by the crazed Belgian.

In fact, looking around I can see loads of little pockets of dodgy dealing going on all over the place; people selling weed, pills, blotters and powders. In the corner, behind the other speaker, a queue has practically formed leading to Ed and Enid. Total drug dustbins, the pair of them. By sunrise all the pills will be sold, bar their personal. The proceeds will be secreted somewhere in their car and they will go and get spectacularly fucked up. They are the bastard sons and daughters of Thatcherism, making their own way in the world, meeting a demand, feeding a market, being self-sufficient, entrepreneurial. All the things we were consciously and subconsciously taught by our politics and culture growing up in the 80s mutated and bastardised for an underculture's needs.

As well as the handful of people selling in bulk like this, there are many more small scale examples of people passing on their high, gifting a half a pill to a friend, or putting something on tick for a mate waiting on a giro. Through the nights tabs are run up, the details of which are promptly forgotten, other than the vague idea that you must owe someone *something*, 'cause you got far more fucked than you could afford to when you went out. Chumpee always says that most of the time he wakes up wondering why he's got no money in his pockets, when he seems to have no drugs left either. Selling pills while on pills is a difficult game to get right, as the urge to give them away, or give them out on tick which is eventually repaid far into the future, is hard to fight.

The problem is: who can say no to a friend when you're buzzing to fuck yourself?

The three Graces are beaming at each other, dancing in a tight circle by the right hand speaker, and I swirl round them for a moment, absorbing their glow, amazed at their collective beauty; Dreads Dave catches me gawping like a schoolboy and we share a laugh about how amazing they look. They widen their circle and we dance with them, trying not to feel like letches, knowing we are totally busted. Blush.

A flash of fire at the back of the warehouse catches my eye and I shuffle to investigate with the littlest Grace, her lush silver trousers and little blond twists shining through the dark as she bounces along, smiling and laughing her way through the crowd. On the edge of a ten feet circle of space we share a spliff and watch a slight bloke with scraggy hair and big trainers shake the excess of flaming petrol from either end of a six foot stick. He starts to spin, the stick circling him, his hand glowing in the light of the fires, his face momentarily visible as the flaming ends flash past it. Slowly at first, on every fourth beat to begin with, he dances; the stick leaves thick blinding trails as he bounces it back and forth, spinning it in front of him. A chunky acidline drops, along with a big lump of looping percussion, and he goes hyper along with it and the crowd; he catches every kickdrum now, he's bang on every beat, the stick moving faster, spinning around his hands, then up above his head, spraying heat and light around him. The afterburn surrounds him like a cocoon, protecting and transforming him. He stops dead as the kickdrum drops out, and plunges the staff ends into a bucket of water at the edge of the crowd. The relative darkness is abrupt and I'm left with huge afterglows on my retinas, reliving the flight of the flames. We whoop our appreciation. Wicked skills freely shared for our entertainment – the warm glow doesn't stop.

Grace and I plunge back into the middle of the crowd, quickly finding a group of friendly faces to surround us; Little My, Nat, Gonzo, Jude, Tash, Welsh Dave and more, more, more. We jabber hellos and find our rhythm, working out how we will share our temporary space together. It doesn't take long, and soon we are spinning around each other seamlessly, laughing cogs in a Heath Robinson machine.
Then the music grinds to a juddering halt.

There is a second of silence before a groan rumbles across

the crowd. Thoughts flash through our collective mind – police finally shutting us down? Overly dramatic DJing? Really shit DJing? Or just the generator out of diesel?

"The lights have gone as well, so it must be the generator," I hear someone say in the half dark.

Nat finally realises the music has stopped, and her dancing gradually slows to a halt. She shakes her head, opens her eyes carefully, as if for the first time in a while, and takes a deep breath.

"You can't stop now," she hollers, loud and clear above the mumbling crowd, "I've just stuck a pill up my bum!"

On cue the lights snap back on and the music grinds into life. Cheers ring around us – for Nat, for the lights, for the music – and within seconds we are back at it at full volume. Nat smiles, happy that her demand has been met. She absent-mindedly punches the air with both hands, shuts her eyes and gets back to her rush.

07 / Wippenberg — Neurodancer

The dust rises.

Several hundred pairs of feet remorselessly stamp it airborne. It mingles with the smoke from a thousand spliffs and hangs in the air, flickering and drifting, illuminated by the fuzzy shaft of sunlight beaming its Sunday morning welcome through the hole in the roof. The sun is up for a glorious day and we are down to basics: music and people and place.

So much more than the sum of its parts.

This is the best bit of a free party. Hours after the clubs have closed, hours before the pubs open, this is the best time. Dignity and seriousness are gladly thrown away and there is comedy dancing, face-pulling and the chatting of shameless gibberish – grown men and women acting like daft kids. We are largely fucked, damaged, people but we have found a fucked, damaged place that feels like home, and we will stay here for as long as we can. There's plenty of room to bounce about for the exhibitionists amongst us and it's finally light enough to see who your fellow dancers are.
    At the back of the warehouse a pile of battered mattresses have appeared from somewhere, and Foxie and Mad Bastard Bob are trampolining back and forth, giggling like Christmas-morning kids. Acid Bob, Abdi and Goon

come in through the double doors and can't resist it, they run and bounce one after another, springing back towards the centre of the dancefloor. Goon misjudges his leap, his depth perception shot to fuck, and hits the floor before his legs are ready. They buckle under him and he ends up a shameless heap, slowly pouring cider over himself. Foxie reaches out a hand to pull him up, crying with laughter.

"M'balance is all skew-wiff, innit, I've only got one flagon," shouts Goon, waving a huge container quarter-full of suspiciously murky liquid, "If I hadn't finished the other one this would be no problem." He smiles then dances off towards the front, aiming for a speaker, any speaker. He knows the dancefloor is still it. The solid line of black and blue boxes has a gravitational pull, from across the site they draw you in. It's still the main reason for being here – the movement, the music. The drugs we could do at home, but here there's a fuck-off soundsystem, loads of friends and space to charge about. That's still what we want, that's why we are still here, why we don't want it to stop. Don't stop, don't make us go home, I want to dance all day. I don't want to stop, don't stop, don't stop. Don't stop the music. Don't stop us dancing.

There are less people here now; our numbers are down to the low hundreds. Just the turbo-nutters left, and those too fucked to get home without help from the turbo-nutters. Spread around the site, everyone moves in time, wherever they are and whatever they are doing. Everyone who is even slightly conscious moves *something*. A line of gouged people slumped on a fucked sofa next to the dancefloor all nod or tap their feet, despite the closed eyes and general air of mong that hangs over them. People are dancing on top of the mounds of rubbish around the edges, and up on the speakerstacks, behind the decks and straight in front, out by the doors and on the roofs of cars. Everyone moves. Loads of smiles shine through the air.

The music has settled into a 150 beats-per-minute rushing-to-fuck cruise, up and down and round and round. Never ending, never resting, always changing. This is Bristol-style techno – the hard, dense kick drums are circled by fine-tuned cymbals and snares, dirty, squelchy, sub-bass notes rumble under our feet, while sweeping strings and swirling acidlines collide up above. The duelling 303's churn away – the deviations flutter up and down; each low rumbling call is answered by a mirroring high squeal. The noises keep spinning off from one another, like a single cell splitting, sub-dividing, splitting, sub-dividing, again and again and again and again and again and again and again and again, getting bigger and more complicated with each addition. The bleeps and the bass ease upwards, the percussion becoming more frantic as the tune lifts us up, making my frontal lobes feel as though they are full of helium.

Fucking chhhhooooooooooooooooooooooooooooonnnnn.

Chumpee spins past, swishing a battered old upright vacuum cleaner around in front of him. He sees my smile and grins back.

"Thought the place could do with a quick scrub up," he says. "And no-one else is gonna do it, so muggins here gets lumbered again!"

The sight of this filthy dreadlocked dropout pretending to tidy an impossibly dusty floor gets me, and I'm helpless with laughter. He slides through the crowd, his trusty piece of broken machinery clearing the dancers out of his way as he pushes piles of dirt from place to place. He goes over to the mong-sofa, and, one-by-one, he makes each swamp-dweller lift their feet so he can hoover beneath them. This confuses them all, very deeply.

The crowd is swelling again, filling the floor – loads of new arrivals are joining us, cars full of people arriving by the look of it. Superb, it's Esther and McKay and Gedge and the rest of the Welsh crew. Most of them are fresh compared to us, and a handful are completely immaculate, as if they have just stepped off a catwalk. An implausibly curvaceous woman in some kind of sailors outfit – with a big white hat and flared white trousers – stomps past and heads straight down the front. Ray and Donna blow kisses as they dance in, still UV'd up from whatever night they were at over the bridge. Hairy munter McKay stops to hug me and Chumpee.

"Had a night in a pub in Chepstow, someone said there was a do over 'yer – glad I came with 'em," he shouts, grinning like a big shaggy muppet, before heading for a speaker.

Fresh legs, fresh smiles; a little buzz hits the dancefloor. Not more drugs, just more people, more of the right people. More of the fuck-ups and weird heads. In a good way.

Tash, Lord Bob, Corrine and me are all enjoying the space at the back of the warehouse, occasionally spinning into the glorious sunshine streaming through the doors, when there's a cheeky little pinch on my arse. I turn to face my gooser and see Zak standing in front of me, grinning. He's wearing his baggy hooded top with a wastedly nonchalant air, his head trying to interact with the solid world around him. He's doing his best but I can see that everything keeps changing and curling on him, sharp edges turning into spongy curves and speech bubbles forming out of other people's words. He's properly, royally, *heroically*, fucked. The old-school LSD that was doing the rounds earlier has left its mark deep in his pupils, which are as clear as the cloudless blue sky above us.

"You OK?" I ask, holding out the spliff I've been slowly smoking to myself.

"Uh... yeah... he he he... um right... fucked – everything's ... y'know..." He looks at me with evangelical zeal, making a sort of chopping motion with his left hand. "Y'know... just bomph... bang on. Spot on. Just, just, *there*. Y'know." There's another sheepish grin.

"Yes mate," I beam at him, "I know."

"Heh. Gotta light?" he asks.

"'Course."

I hold it out, shielding the flame from the slight breeze. He looks at his hands. Dirty fingers hold smokables in both of them; what looks like a very ragged roll-up, fat and falling apart, in one and the remains of the spliff I just passed him in the other. Both are having all the life and shape squeezed out of them as he concentrates on communicating, concentrates on not just sitting down and watching the stunning colours flashing before his eyes.

He can't decide what to light so he sparks both of them, taking huge drags on each, grinning a heartfelt smile in our general direction. An acid-drenched smile, glowing in the sun. He takes another massive drag of both and coughs the smoke straight back up. He looks at us with watery eyes, smiles his big grin again, and then crosses his arms and bimbles off, mumbling a goodbye as he goes. Both the spliff and the rollup go out, instantly forgotten. Tash laughs and passes me the spliff she's smoking, to replace the one I've just lost. We dance on.

I'm sitting with Little My, skinning up, flirting, sinking together into the sofa on the edge of the dancefloor. Our heads are slumped temple to temple so she can crack me

up, ripping the piss out of munters staggering past us. Next to us Gollum is completely unconscious; people have started piling things on him.

Not in a nasty way.

In an *artistic* way.

His shoulders are supporting arrangements of crushed cans and empty vodka bottles, and on his head a four-high stack of Stella cans wobbles every time he breathes. Foxie is trying to get a cider bottle to balance on his knee, but can't because he's laughing so much.

Jude stomps past, closely followed by Zak, floating like a tethered balloon. She glances at us and grins, checking behind her to make sure she hasn't lost him.

"Have you seen Brenda recently?" she asks. We shake our heads. She laughs and points into the heart of the dancefloor before continuing on her way, Zak close behind her.

There's Brenda, slap-bang in the middle of the floor, dancing as if it is the only thing she has ever known. She only did her first pill last night, for her birthday. Jude brought her round, Chumpee sorted her out, and there she is still going strong, red jeans caked to the knees in dust, cardigan hanging halfway down her back, face drenched in sweat, hands smeared with dirt. She looks amazing, simply because of the smile on her face. She glows.

"Look at the state of that," says Little My, pointing to the scene developing at the edge of the decks. Jammer's playing a chunky techno set, swaying and laughing but holding it down. There's a spliff clamped between his teeth, he's holding a record in one hand and punching the air with the other, totally on a roll; his partner in crime, Sophie, is giving him the eye from just in front of the right-hand speaker. Completely shitfaced, Jasper's standing a few feet away, holding a tall geezer up with one hand and waving a record in Jammer's face with the other. The tall geezer has a got a proper wobble on – the record bag over one shoulder is making it difficult for him to balance, and he's waving his can of brew around as he stumbles from foot to foot, trying to stay upright on the shit-covered floor

Jasper finally gives up on hassling Jammer and gets chatting to Eddie instead. Even from here we can tell by the way Jasper keeps waving his arms that Wobbler is the best DJ we'll ever hear and, in Jasper's humble-but-obviously-correct opinion, Eddie should bump Jammer off the decks so he can have a play. Eddie gives him a 'nothing to do with me mate, I just bring the speakers' smile and get back to racking out lines. Jasper turns to Jammer again and shouts so loud we can hear him from ten feet away:

"Jus' play ma fucccking record man, c'mooooonnn!"

Jammer gives in; he smiles indulgently at Jasper, shouts something to Eddie about needing a piss anyway, then shoves the headphones into Wobblers hands, who has slumped onto a pile of pallets, half asleep. He gurns *so* hard as he looks at the headphones in his hand that I think he going to lose his jaw over his left shoulder. He's hauled up by Jasper, then makes the record that's playing jump by slamming his can on the table next to the decks

"Looking good," I shout to Little My.

"Is it fuck!" she shouts back.

She's right of course. It looks dreadful. Jasper is giving it loads with a huge smile on his face, while Wobbler does a dreadful galloping-horses mix to get out of Jammer's last tune. Eddie, bless him, instinctively leans back to get the finished record out of Wobblers grubby hands and puts it safely in Jammer's bag. The dancers, evenly spread through the room, falter a bit but get their collective rhythm back as the next tune kicks in. Jasper was right; it's a banging tune, well worth playing. Less sure about his DJ though.

Wobbler really is very tall, and he has to bend down a long way to get to the decks; he leans so far forward to peer at the record that's playing, that I think he's just going to lie his head on the spinning vinyl.

"Ooooooooh," I say, "This is going downhill fast."

He swings round to his left to reach for his record bag, and it all goes wrong immediately. His head spins and he stumbles backwards away from the 1210s, trips over a cable and falls on his arse. Flailing and grabbing as he goes down, he manages to pull the whole set-up off the table and onto the floor around him – decks, mixer, can of brew, everything. The music screeches to a tearing halt, and shouts of disapproval shoot up from the crowd. A raging Eddie leaps up, nostrils caked in gak, and flicks a switch to cut the horrendous noise through the speakers. Jasper is fucking mortified, as is Wobbler. They scrabble around trying to get everything back onto the table, Wobbler being more of a hindrance than a help.

Ray and Donna are by the back doors the whole time, utterly bolloxed, eyes closed and blissfully dancing to the fluctuating hum of the generator out the back.

Little My and I are crying with laughter when Jammer walks back in.

"What did I miss?" he shouts at us – we can barely talk through the tears.

A few minutes later there is a hum, and the gratifying sound of a kickdrum thumps back into the room. Jammer just smiles as he lines up his next tune.

Out, into the blue skies and brilliant sunshine. There are loads of people around the place in various states of disrepair, slumped in corners, perched on pallets. Fuck, it's hot; feel that sun. Chumpee and Caspar are blatantly on a mission, storming around chatting to all the dodgiest people on site, rounding them up into a corner in the shade, just inside the warehouse doors. Chumpee catches my eye and performs a wobbly wink, beckoning me over. Little My and Rez are busy polishing a huge, three foot long broken piece of mirror, using any piece of rag they can find, including their own increasingly filthy clothes. I sit and skin up, watching the moment of spontaneous organization and generosity take shape.

The crew crowding together all either sell drugs, or just have pockets full of them for personal consumption, and a large pile of pills quickly forms – ten, fifteen, twenty, more. One or two people empty out wraps of coke or MDMA instead. Chumpee and Caspar both give generous donations before getting to work crushing the pills; Little My helps, all of them flattening the multi-coloured collection of drugs as best they can, with credit cards, lighters, the flat of a knife that appears from somewhere. Little My then starts obsessively chopping at the finest stuff with hyper fast hand movements using a razor blade that Caspar fishes out from his keks. Slowly a huge mound of off-white powder forms in the middle of the mirror. She starts to make lines, big fat chunky ones, as she goes through it, using about half before she runs out of room on the shiny surface. Spliff finished I dance round them with Rez, the pair of us peering over the circled heads every now and then and threatening to sneeze, to general disapproval.

Chumpee, Little My and Caspar begin walking around the dance floor, mirror held aloft, doing their best to give a line of pill to everyone who wants one. It takes two to hold the mirror, while the other one sorts out the note and tells people what's what.

"Yes, mate – want a line?" Chumpee asks munter after munter. It's one of the funniest things I've ever seen, the faces already fucked people pull when this trio of gorgeous grinning freaks appear in front of them offering them free drugs. Tash runs to her truck and gets some straws when the note starts to get a bit soggy, and Donna and Ray follow the mirror round, offering drinks of water as it moves on. Me and Rez dance in big circles around them all, every now and then stomping closer, giving whoever is holding the mirror a blowback from our big fat strong spliff.

The DJ and all the crew behind the decks are sorted out, and there is a brief pause as more pills and powders are added to the pile. Extra lines are chopped and we head through the back doors. There are whole sets of people out here that I haven't seen for hours; Helen and Norm, Ramona and Jude and loads more, are sat around a fire under the flyover, chatting and laughing. They appreciate a little pick-me-up as much as anyone.

Inside the warehouse the effect is palpable; a shared chemical reaction floods in, a surge of energy rushes through. People come back into the room to snort their lines and have a stomp, tired legs ready for one last blowout. The dancefloor starts to expand again as the party gets its second wind. The crowd done, Chumpee, Caspar, and everyone who contributed gather together at the back of the room. The rest of the powder is divided into the appropriate number of obscenely fat lines, and is caned in no time at all. A job well done. Everyone happy.

I only manage to do half of mine before handing the straw to Little My to finish it for me, my eyes watering and nose blocked with powder. I decide to enjoy my rush from the comfort of a bassbin, so I pass my dope to Chumpee with a smile.

"Skin up and meet me down the front."

08 / Starpower – Renegade 303

I'm flying again.

The music's gone nicely weird and we're spinning and grinning, fucked and flirting, wasted and wobbling. Slow crisp breakbeats cut through the murk of the grimy, churning techno. A sharp acidline bursts into life, midrange at first, before racing up through the trebles to an ear-achingly high pitch. Zak and I lock eyes across the dancefloor as it soars and screeches – we both know this is the kind of thing that presses all the right buttons – we dance and laugh at each other through the haze. Twenty feet away in another direction Chumpee punches the air and points at us, laughing his head off watching us go for it. Somehow the three of us dance together even though we are nowhere near each other, connections lazering across the room from fried synapse to fried synapse, a glowing triangle of fucked-up-ness that zings between us. What a fucking record; it only does one thing but it does it fucking perfectly and we let our DJ know it. I don't know who she is but she looks well happy with her killer tune, flicking the deck off and letting the remnants of the sparse drum pattern grind to a halt among rapturous applause. She presses 'Start' on the other deck, smiling a confident smile; the next record is lined up in the right spot, ready to go, and the deep beats and high sounds of a stone-cold classic drop. Collective muscle-memory from a thousand previous dances kicks in and we scream in delight – we know every beat, every bleep, every boom. When those swooping, chiming, chords rush in we are lifted as one. We go with it, letting the richness and warmth of the music dictate our tone, drawing the hugs out of us, revelling in the early morning sun. Up up up.

Feel the love.

I'm suddenly aware of a pair of blue uniforms in the corner of my eye. I'm not, as I first think, hallucinating – there really are two policemen shuffling through the manky warehouse, avoiding people's stares and trying not to be bounced into by the spaced-out dancers skanking in a world of their own. They eventually make it through the crowd to the decks, as people wander in from the sunshine to see what's going on, determined to dance defiantly in the face of such a meagre police presence. Me, Casper and Goon unconsciously drift closer to the decks.

The senior officer, wincing as huge kickdrums crash around him, leans over the mixer towards Hog, who is utterly fucked, DJing back-to-back with Stan. Hog looks up and grins. The officer shouts something, but the music stomps all over his voice as the sound tumbles out of his mouth, making him mute before a wall of noise. Hog cups one hand around his ear, gives an exaggerated shrug and gets back to his mix. Even from where we are we can hear the copper shouting:

"*Turn it off, scumbag!*"

Hog looks at him again and, with another over-the-top 'I don't understand' shrug, turns up the volume. The pounding beats drop for a minute, leaving just a dirty bassline, weird rolling chimes, and a growing snare-roll. The voice of a crazed evangelical preacher starts to loop over and over, getting louder and louder:

"... the world of God, the world of God, the world of God, the world of God..."

A beat's worth of silence.

"**Come With ME.**"

On the '**ME**' we go wild. The 4/4 crunches into place, the rumble turns into a scream, and we fucking have it; cheering and shouting, obnoxious in the face of authority. The older policeman's face turns red in the crash of a cymbal.

Eddie has finally noticed that the pigs are here, and tries to get the senior officer away from the decks (and away from Stan who, oblivious to everything, has just sparked up a fat hash pipe). The younger copper is lost, staring at Rez, Dot and Little My dancing in front of him, dirty, beautiful, crazy. For a moment his jaw just hangs open, until he is brought back with a quick kick from his passing superior.

Another wicked churner comes on as Eddie escorts the two policemen towards the doors out; just a dense-as-fuck kickdrum and a deep grinding 303. We shout and cheer at their departing backs, cries of 'oink, oink' and 'wankers' flying though the air. They look somehow dejected and furious as they get into their squad car and pull away. Everyone immediately starts to skin up, or gets out a bag of pills and necks another one, or starts chopping a line on an amp stack. The surge of cheeky adrenaline gives the party another little kick up the arse.

I wander back out into the sunshine with Dreads Dave, and we slump onto a pile of rubble in the shade from the sagging corrugated roof; a big circle of people are deep into a tripping, tangent-filled conversation, telling police stories.

"To be honest," says Enid, "they got off lightly. I've been at parties where they've been given a much harder time. D'you remember that solstice party near Abergavenny?"

"Was that the lone copper on a bike?" Goon chips in. "Mad Bastard Bob following him all round site asking him if he wanted some Special Brew, shaking a manky can full of, full of... *gob* in his face?"

"Yeah, that one," says Enid. "He kept shouting, 'You can finish it, I've got more!' didn't he. And do you remember – in the end those lairy women started touching up the copper and stroking his jacket, touching him up and taking the piss, then yanked his trousers down! Fucking shown up. He buggered off quick sharp."

"Yeah, everyone was singing the stripping song at him," says Goon, "Or was that somewhere else?"

"No, I think that was that quarry party," says Chumpee, "the one where Nat and Hog changed into each others clothes for some reason. And then walked out from behind a bush as two pigs walked up to the party behind them."

"Oh yeah. I don't know who jumped more when they turned round," laughs Acid Bob, "Hog when he realised there was a copper behind him, or the constable when he realised the one in the dress had a massive fucking beard!" He giggles at the memory as he slowly struggles to his wobbly feet and hands each of us a blotter.

"Right," he says. "Tea run! Who wants a cuppa?"

Concentrating really hard he wades through the munters towards the Big Purple Tea Van parked just inside the warehouse doors, carefully holding his fingers out; three fingers on his left hand equals three with sugar, four on the right means four without.

The conversation rambles gently on until McKay mutters, "Here he comes then. 'Ow many of them teas are gonna make it, d'you reckon?"

Bob is carrying seven steaming polystyrene cups, balanced on a knackered tray. His walking is all kinds of fucked-up. The navigational computing required to keep the tray level, walk on the uneven ground *and* avoid the other munters staggering about is enormous. Not one of us moves to help him because we are too busy laughing, and we know we wouldn't do any better.

Eventually, like a great explorer making it across the frozen tundra, he reaches us and passes the teas around.

"When I was in the queue I got an itch, and scratched it," he says, "then realised I didn't know what I was doing with sugars. So I thought 'fuck it' and just got seven mushroom teas instead. Is that alright?"

We all laugh. The beerboys who had said 'no thanks' to tea suddenly take an interest, and the hot earthy liquid is shared between us all. It's a bit difficult to get down to be honest, but it's mushroom tea, who can say no?

God only knows where the conversation starts but the first words I hear come from Goon who grins at whatever Acid Bob has just said, and replies:

"... yeah, yeah, Shaven Monkey Monthly!"

This makes them both fall about. The conversation spins off into tangents about apes and monkeys.

"I like mandrills," says Acid Bob.

"Weird looking fuckers," says Chumpee.

"Did you know," Bob continues, "that mandrills can bend six inch nails between their thumb and forefinger?" He holds his hand up and mimes the action.

Gonzo looks up from the spliff he's building, "Where the fuck do they get the *nails* from? In the middle of the fucking *jungle*?" he asks.

There's laughter from everyone, including Bob. Just as it subsides Gonzo looks up again.

"Is someone teaching them woodwork?"

And we're gone, crying with laughter.

We're still chuckling and shouting jokes at each other when Grant comes storming up the sloped pavement towards us, utterly fucked, eyes bulging out of his head. He's waving a long thin plank in one hand and shouting.

"I'm such a special person; I'm such a special person."

He really means it.

In one smooth movement he leans the plank at a forty-five degree angle against the pile of pallets supporting the clumped roof above our heads and, still shouting about how wonderful he is, he kicks the plank in half. A few of us glance up to check the roof isn't going to collapse on our heads before shouting back.

"Yeah Grant, you're a pillar of strength."

"A beacon in the darkness."

"You give hope to us all."

He laughs and looks at us, suddenly utterly deadpan.

"That's right," he says, "You. Are. Right."

He nods and staggers off across the carpark shouting, "I'm such a special person!" at everyone who passes. We watch him pinball over to another seated circle, and then onto another.

Goon stands up. "Time fer a dance, I reckon."

We all agree and pile back onto the dancefloor, which is suddenly looking very sparse. Down the front in acres of space Little My, Rez and Dot are having a lovely time. There's a classic tune coming in, breakbeat techno, nice, skippy, bouncy drum patterns but a dark, underlying churn that stops it feeling like fluff.

I feel wankered again.

The beats drop out; there is a leave-a-message 'beeeeep' followed by a distant woman's voice, upset, unsettling:

> "P-p-pick up the phone now... you couldn't even **say it**, you couldn't even **tell me**, and you **won't** even pick up the **phone**"

There's a pause, the acid builds, and then she shouts:

> "You're such a **bastard** and a **liar!**"

Everything crashes back in, beats clattering around,

screaming noises going berserk. A small voice somewhere deep in the mix says, "Oh no," then there's another 'beeeep' and its back into the voice sample, spooky synth lines swirling around the words.

Little My is only a few feet away from us but is oblivious to our presence, dancing like a whirling dervish, mouthing the words to herself, shouting along.

"*You're such a bastard and a liar!*" she screams, smiling to herself as she lurches forwards, the bassdrums hammering back into her ears. She is dancing on the edge of delirium, in the grey area between standing up and falling over, eyes shut tight, limbs flailing, no thought for those around her. She doesn't care, she has to express herself, has to fill all the available space; she doesn't mind if she stomps on toes with her spraypainted silver DMs.

She's wicked.

They all are.

Dot, with her single long twist of hair from just above her temple, locked into a munted stomp, beating back the sound through sheer force of will, and Rez gliding in circles around them, grinning and smiling at her younger companions, happy at their happiness. They smile back, in return happy at her happiness at their happiness. Now, that's the right kind of feedback loop to be locked into; we whoop and swirl as we join them, wanting to share in their glow.

09 / New Order – Confusion
(Pump Panel Reconstruction)

Fuck, my head's spinning. Really fucking spinning.

Wwwhaauugh,

Blergh.

I feel like shit all of a sudden. What the fuck?
> Deep breaths.
> Come on.
> Where am I?
> What's happening?

Where am I?

Think.

It all started with that German geezer.
    I'd drunk that mushy tea, had a wicked little dance, and dropped something else at some point. He was a friend of Caspar's, and had turned up at about 4am, inching through the crowd on his huge olive-green, demonic-looking bike, parking it beside the speakerstacks before stomping on the spot next to it for an hour. I ended up sitting with him, Karl I think he said his name was, talking about drugs,

music and the bike, of course, with its massive handlebars, monstrous misshapen fuel tank held on with gaffer, and tires so chunky they could be used for a Mars mission. I'd never met him before, but we had been getting on quite well, sharing a spliff, chatting away, when he'd suddenly started laughing and walked off. Caspar had looked at my confused face and laughed as well.

"What were you talking about?" he'd asked me.

"Dunno really, drugs and music and that?" I'd replied.

"I didn't know you understood German?" he'd said.

"What? I can't understand German? Barely understand English."

"Hahahaha. Karl is German…"

"I know that."

"… and he understands a little bit of English, but doesn't really speak it. He's been talking to you in German for the last ten minutes."

"Fuck. Off. Has he fuck."

"Honest dude. Would I lie to you?" His face told me the truth.

That totally, *totally*, did my head in.

"What was he saying?" I'd asked. "You speak German, don't you?"

"I missed the start of it," he told me, chuckling away. "I caught a bit where he said something like 'you don't understand me do you?' and 'Bist du zu?' – 'Are you fucked? – something like that."

"Really? Really really?"

Caspar had nodded and repeated, "Bist du zu. Are you fucked. Yeah." He gave me a squeeze on the arm and offered me his beer. I declined the warm brew and decided to roll a spliff.

Well, I tried to roll a spliff.

My fat sausagey fingers couldn't sort out the skins, then something dripped on it and soaked the baccy, then I couldn't get my lighter to work or the hash to crumble, I couldn't get a grip in the papers so just folded it in half. Then I had no saliva – so dry, so dry. A tongue like scorched cactus bark, stuck to the roof of my mouth. I spent ages chewing the inside of my cheeks, finally rasping my tongue across the top of the skins. At which point I realised that I had them the wrong way up, with the sticky bit at the bottom, and the whole thing just crumbled in my hands and ended at my feet.

That was not a good sign.

I can always skin up.

Always.

I staggered off to try to have a dance instead, giving my lump of pot to Caspar as I went, asking him to skin up for me.

So.

That's where I am.

That's where I am.

Here.

Here I am.

Here I am, spinning out.

I feel skuzzy. A cold sweat. I wipe my hand across my damp cheek, something tickling me there. A thin streak of orange goo comes off my face and onto my hand.

What the fuck is that?

Everything around me is dirty; a thick layer of dust and sweat coats every surface of this derelict place. You can see why it was abandoned. It's a fucking shithole. A dump. I shiver involuntarily; my stomach churns and a bile-thick burp lurches up my gullet, burning in the back of my throat.

Boy, I feel fucking rough. Have a dance. Just have a dance.

My head rocks back and forward, ready to fall off my shoulders and roll across the brown fetid floor. Someone I don't recognise glares at me, their jaw spooning unnaturally round the side of their head. His eyes stay put, but the rest of his face twists and turns. What the fuck is wrong with his face? Was he disabled? Is that just me, was that me, or was his face really deformed?

Fuckfuckfuck… have a dance have a dance have a dance…

No.

Dancing isn't working either.

The music's too harsh, too discordant. Practically gabba, no depth, just banging away. Clang clang clang fucking clang. Worse, it's too loud for the speakers, distorting like fuck at the edges. A nasty sound. My legs are heavy beneath me, dragging me down. My feet are stuck in place, and I just jerk back and forward, weakly punching one arm in front of me. I force myself to close my eyes, to try and lose myself in the music, but there is nowhere to go with it, it's just a shallow noise, no complexity, no subtlety, no pop, no style.

I dance half-heartedly for what feels like hours.

When I grab a look at someone's watch I can see it has only been minutes. I can feel a thin-lipped grimace spreading across my face, taut and curling down at the edges, the tension in my body leaking from my pores, souring my space. People stare at me with black eyes. No eyelashes, no whites, no pupils. Just big, black pits staring at me.

Some big geezer, short but wide, tensed neck tendons barely strapping his bulging head to his shoulders, stands in front of me and just shouts in my face for a few minutes.

I cannot understand a word he is saying.

Is he going to punch me?

No?

Yes?

Don't know.

His massive misshapen hands flex in and out of fists. He's got shit tattoos all over the right side of his torso, spiders' webs, and blue veined bulbous women, spindly tigers and wilted roses. Built like a brick shithouse, his ugly, flecked mouth twists as he growls and howls. I can't help but just stare blankly back as he shouts in my face. His eyes are black, no iris at all, the whites so veined with red that they look like puddles of blood. They're bulging; the pressure behind his eyes pushing them out of the sockets.

His.

Whole.

Body.

Straining.

Like he's having a *massive* shit.

This slow-motion thought makes me half-smile for some reason, which provokes him to prod my chest, pushing me back on my heels. He's disgusting. What a fucking horrible, horrible wanker. I stare open mouthed.

He jabs me in the chest again with a long-nailed finger, and I stagger backwards. I shake my head, and furrow my brow at him, stepping back again. He steps forward, pushing me again. He's massive. Even though I'm taller than him he seems to fill the whole of my field of vision, looming over me, surrounding me on all sides.

Fuckfuckfuckfuckfuckfuck.

What shall I do?

I can't fight. Why does he want to fight?

Does he want to fight?

Why? What have I done? I can't move, I just can't move at all.

Fuckfuckfuckfuckfuckfuckfuckfuckfuckfuckfuckfuck.

Caspar appears, handing me my lump of pot which I immediately drop. He scoops it up for me, waving the burning spliff in his hand. He grins at the gabba dude, and does a nod at him which somehow manages to convey the message: "What's up? You look interesting. I fight if I have to, you know?". Cas leans in to listen to what he is shouting, then shouts something back over the grinding music, and raises the fat, smoking joint. He puts the burning end into his mouth and leans towards the geezer. The Gabba Munter laughs and takes the blowback. Cas pulls the glowing end out of his mouth, gives it a bit of a blow to check it's burning evenly, then shoves it back in. He leans in and blows a huge amount of smoke down my throat. It feels like it is drifting out of my ears, I'm so full. I cough and splutter and try to say thank you but no words come out, just a strangled collection of vowels and consonants. He laughs, pats my back, and dances off, looking back as he moves around, keeping an eye on Gabba Munter, who's chilled a bit, and is stomping a few feet away, oblivious to my presence.

What the fuck was that all about.

Fucking hell.

What just happened?

Fuck, this music is fucking shit. My guts rumble again, my sphincter suddenly getting involved, tensing and relaxing. What the fuck. Do I need a shit? I don't need a shit do I?

Fuckfuckfuck. Just dance, just dance for a bit. It'll pass.

My guts churn again.

Just try to dance.

I try not to stumble as I walk up the ramp under the corrugated roof into the other warehouse, stepping over half-dead bodies curled in the now grey morning light. The sky has clouded over, and taken away the shine this place had. I'm scrabbling in my pockets for a couple of scraps of tissue. I know I had a few pieces earlier. Found them. The empty warehouse stinks of piss, dark grey marks visible in waist high lines along the breezeblock walls, puddling to the floor.

I fucking retch. My guts churn again. Am I really going to try and find somewhere to have a shit? I flashback to Castlemorton, climbing through some shrubs trying to find somewhere to go – day three I think, and it felt like I had no choice – only to emerge from the undergrowth to see a field of turds, each topped by a few delicate scraps of pink tissue paper fluttering in the breeze. The thought stops me dead in my tracks. Now, as then, I decide to clench and hold it.

I tiptoe through the debris and back to the dancefloor, uncomfortable, spinning inside my own head. Where is everyone? Can't see anyone I want to sit with. I half-heartedly stomp around, too tense to dance. Too tense to dance. Too tense to dance. Too tense to dance.

I get stuck in loops in my head. Thinking about bad things I have done, bad things people have done to me. Thinking about bad things.

Someone is playing a bit of jungle, complex rhythms stinging my ears, raw basslines distorting though the speakers. An alien, insect noise roars out; I can see Nina in front of the speaker giving it loads, blond plaits and blue dress flapping, arms bouncing in front of her. Her reaction tells me the tune must have something special going on, but I'm too fucked to find it. I don't mind a bit of jungle

usually but not now, please not now. It's just too much.

The bedraggled bodies left on the floor look ugly as fuck. Twisted faces, gurned out and scabby. Grey, potholed skin taut over skeletal features. Minging clothes and haloed nostrils everywhere. I catch a glimpse of my reflection in a car window and I look even worse. Cavernous black bags under my eyes. White flecks of dried spittle around my mouth. Scratches and acne sprawled across my skin. I can't help but shudder again.

The music somehow feels worse than a moment ago. It takes a while for me to work it out, but I slowly begin to understand that there is a car parked in front of me, about twenty feet back from the decks, smack in the middle of the dance floor. It's full of ket-heads beeping the horn repeatedly, regularly, just off of the beat, just out of time. That's what is currently destroying the music.

I lurch back and forth, trying to find a rhythm in the conflicting noises echoing round the bare warehouse, a kickdrum clashing with the car horn. I get closer to the speakers, trying to drown out the incessant fucking racket from across the floor. I see Eddie and Marty leaning in the window of the car, trying their best to persuade them to fuck off. They are ignored.

Dancing still isn't working.

I sit by the dancefloor on a pile of rubble, next to Ramona, who I used to live with in the flat above Ruby. Janice is sprawled across the apex of the rubble, unconscious, an empty bottle of Jack clutched in one hand, burnt out fag-butt in the other. Mona gives me a little hug as I sit down, but she sits ever-so-slightly turned the other way. I spin inside my head again, wondering if I have pissed her off, if she is blanking me. She keeps on chatting and flirting with this bloke. I recognise him now, from the pub, pretty boy, student, new in town. Got a good dark look going on. She's had her eye on him for a few weeks now.

My head spins.

I find her hand resting on the pile of bricks next to mine and grab hold of it. This helps. She smiles at me when I take her hand, but keeps talking to Pretty Boy. He laughs and leans closer to her. She laughs some more. My head spins again.

Maybe I have really pissed her off. What if she's really cross? Wish I could think of something to say. Without realising I squeeze her hand harder and tighter and tighter and harder, until she suddenly jumps in pain and turns to look at me.

"You alright honey? That hurts."

She loosens her hand from my grip, as I mumble a noise that is meant to be sorry, but doesn't quite get there. She gives me a hug and looks worried. I can't articulate anything, so give her a peck on the cheek and stagger off, back towards the dancefloor.

Time warps around me.

It takes me about three days to smoke the fag Ramona gives me as I leave. I spend about two weeks trying to check my pockets, taking stuff out and then putting it back again, for a while convinced I've lost my hash, for a while convinced I've lost all my money, for a while convinced I've lost my key. For a while I'm convinced I've lost *something*, without being quite sure what it is.

The music washes around me, huge phased vocals circling up and down, in and out of earshot, the words always threatening to come into focus but never actually making themselves heard. My head spins with it, still unsure where it is. My body doesn't feel like mine. It feels like I've borrowed it from someone else, like its a few sizes too small. It feels like the music is shouting my name, in amongst the swirling noises. I ignore it.

Why would my name be in a tune?

I stand and listen for hours to the same looping four-beats of clattered percussion, my name being repeated over and over again, deep down in the mix of noise.

I'm frozen.

Caspar appears, shouting "Bert" and waving a spliff in front of me. He grins and hands it to me, shouts "Bert" again and gives me an overenthusiastic punch on the arm. The sudden pain draws my brain back in, just a little. I try to mumble a thank you, but I don't think anything comes out.

I try to get onto the beat, conscious again of the honking fucking cocks sat in their car, still just out of time but still painfully regular, enjoying the attention. Quite a few people are gathered around the car now, shouting and pointing towards the warehouse doors, getting increasingly irate. Whoever's playing works the system, turning it up, trying to drown them out.

Inside the car they just laugh, and rack out more huge lines of ketamine, thick lumps of it dropping back out of their noses, eyes bulging and faces reddening; disappearing down a hole. Whoever it is sitting in the driver's seat laughs and hammers the roof of the car, then just stretches out his hand and braces himself hard against the car's horn. The long dead tone sweeps across the warehouse and fills it to the ceiling with shit.

Eddie shouts "Fucking cunts" as loud as he can at the window, then stalks away, back to the rig, back to the amps, trying to block them out of his mind. A few more people around the car shout too, but they slowly drift away from the dirty metal box, leaving it to its incessant drone.

Everything is so snarled up and tightly wound, my head feels like it is in a vice, being squeezed by the pressure.

I stagger through the doors behind the speakers, to the car park behind the warehouse. One of the pillars that hold up the dual carriageway sits fat and grey the other side of the still smouldering bonfire. The towering underside of the road is bleak and oppressive; the constant rumble of traffic feels like an earthquake. The sheer otherworldliness of it is too imposing and intimidating for my fragile mind.

I don't know where to go.

Gonzo, skinning up by the fire, sees me come flailing out of the door and calls me over to him. I go and join the circle; its him, a few of his mates from Manchester that I don't really know, Helen who I used to live with, and a few other faces I recognise but have never spoken to. What could I say to them? What can I talk about? What do I know?

There's a big gap in the circle of people sat around the fire, so I plonk myself there, fumbling for stuff to skin up with, trying to pretend that there's nothing wrong with me, trying to pretend I'm normal. The smouldering fire coughs smoke all over me, drifting constantly in my direction. This must be why there is a space where I am now sitting.

I stare at my feet.

I realise I've been holding my breath for too long and instinctively inhale. I choke and splutter, not knowing what to do. Gonzo saves me from myself, calling me right next to him, shoving people up to make a space for me to squeeze in.

He grins, and whispers, "Alright Bert. You ok lovely, what's up?"

I just grimace in return, unable to persuade my frontal lobes, lungs and tongue to cooperate enough for me to speak. My mind is stuck in a loop of indecision, frozen by infinite options, unable to process overwhelming sensations. He gives me a concerned smile and pulls me in, putting an arm around my shoulder. "Sit with me for a bit."

Someone asks me a question while I am shuffling my hands through my pockets, trying to sort out skins and pot and tobacco, a feat of planning and dexterity that is still beyond me. I look blankly at the questioner, unable to process the collection of seemingly random Northern sounds. Even if I knew what they had said, their accent thick and impenetrable to me, I have no idea how I would work out a reply. Gonzo just leans forward and starts a long rambling story about their Manchester days.

"Gis'yer pot," he mumbles to me, and in a few short minutes he rolls me a big strong hash spliff. I'm so grateful it's untrue.

"I don't know if I want to pass this on," I whisper back to him a few minutes later. I realise these are the first words I have been able to say for an hour or more and smile. It's been an ugly hour. The thick brown smoke is weighing me down, pulling me down, reattaching my head to the rest of my body.

He grins and rolls another one for himself, his eyes half-closed, and his beaming smile spreading from ear to ear. One of his long, strong, thin arms stretches around my shoulders and pulls me in again; we smile at each other and simultaneously blow smoke towards the fire. He burbles nonsense to me, telling me stories, telling me jokes, taking the piss out of munters staggering past. Never giving my brain time to spin off on its own. The sound of the car horn from inside the warehouse stops at some point, noticeable by its absence. The music becomes a point of potential rather than despair.

Slowly but surely, I begin to think that things might be back on track.

10 / Technohead – The Passion

It's getting late.

Its time to think about leaving, time to try and make some decisions about re-entry into the real world. Where next? Home, pub, park, a random front room? Fuck knows. Working out exactly where we are going and who is doing what is going to take a fair bit of thought and coordination – collectively and individually.

After my ugly hour I've had another lovely little dance, an excellent little shuffle. I haven't scaled the heights of the middle of the night but it got the blood flowing in the right directions again. I'm still feeling a bit tender round the synapses, but I'm doing ok.

Thank fuck for Gonzo. Thank fuck for dancing.

A big crowd of us are milling just outside the warehouse, starting to burn in the hot noon sun. Zak, Goon and Jasper are supposed to be doing a few hours work today but they are well late; they should have started at a video duplication warehouse at ten, labelling and packing videos by hand. It's as utterly mind-numbing as it sounds, and shit money, but its cash in hand and just about survivable when we're stoned and gouging in the middle of the week. Now though, this extra Sunday morning shift is looking like an impossible dream. The three of them keep staring at each other and dissolving into giggles, everything going unsaid but totally understood.

A very strange man is taking his dog for a Sunday

morning walk over the bypass, with its six lanes of constant traffic. He pauses and looks down at us from fifty feet up; Goon notices him and waves his can. "OI MATE, MATE, 'ERE MATE," he shouts, getting his attention, "DDOOOOOOO MMYYYYYY SSSHHIIIIIFFFFT**TT**!"

The strange man peers down, then pulls his head back over the side, confused by the vision of loveliness hollering at him. Jasper, Zak and the rest of us laugh 'til it hurts, echoing the cry every time the bloke becomes visible again through a gap in the concrete walls above us.

"You alright, Jasper," I ask, "had a good night? Haven't seen you for hours."

"Yeah Bert, wicked one, wicked one," he says, "I lost my coat for about three hours, and then stood on it while I was dancing by a speaker. How lucky was that?"

"That explains the uh, the uh, footprints on the back, up yer back."

"Yeah… and I puked on someone."

"What?"

"I puked on someone. Just as well I haven't really eaten anything since we went to the Tropic Club on Wednesday. Is it Sunday now? It's Sunday, innit? Don't know if I can face a roast dinner."

"Mate, stop talking about food and tell me what happened."

"Well, I was kind-of sexy dancing with this girl, she was lovely, one of the Welsh lot I think, and we were flirting a bit. I took a massive glug of my beer for the first time in ages, while she was doing a little twirl in front of me, dancing in a little circle, all elegant and that. The beer was fucking rank – warm and flat – and my guts just went Fuck. Off. It came straight back out again. Only liquid, y'know. Not much of it, but enough to go all over the back of her pristine white blouse."

"Ouch," I say, "what did you do?"

"I just ran away, shouting sorry, before she worked out

what happened," he says, scuffing dust sheepishly from place to place with his feet.

There is an explosion of laughter from the floor by our ankles, Goon is suddenly rolling helplessly in the dust, being tickled by Polly, her bright red hair and multi-coloured outfit in sharp contrast to his filthy shaved head and irredeemably dirty clothes. Zak looks at Chumpee, who's been sorting out the work for us with the bloke who owns the business.

"I can't go to work. No way, no way. I can barely see," he says.

Chumpee smiles,"Don't blame you mate."

They bump heads and try to work out a plan, and I wander with Nina. She's looking for her flatmate Bruce, who she hasn't seen since dawn. He might not even still be here, but she wants to have one last check before she chips off with us. I think she's got half an eye on Chumpee. We stagger arm in arm around the outside of the warehouse, stepping over the dirty, happy people sprawled in the dust soaking up the sun. The music is still pulsing out of the rig, giving a lovely rhythm to walking, talking, nodding. It's changed again, into funky, slinky, deep, deep house, DIY style.

The bursting blood-vessel-red shaved skull of Red Kenny is lolling backwards out of the open side doors of a big blue coach. If it wasn't for the unearthly glowing colour in his cheeks and forehead you would think he was dead from the look of the rolled back head, the slack jaw, and the huge white halos around each nostril. The coach is a monstrosity in itself, a huge silver wagon with the top half of a Volkswagen camper welded onto the roof, making it nearly as tall as a double-decker bus. Nina and I totter past and as we do Kenny drags himself up, looking as if his neck is double jointed. There are loads of munters sat cross-legged in the semi-darkness of the coach beyond his feet. They're Kenny's crew, a bunch of lairy cunts mainly, some of them the same ones who were parked on the dancefloor earlier. In the middle of them all is a Baby-Blu camping stove and a shiny collection of saucepans, next to which is a transparent bottle, half full of liquid. The label says 'Rose Water', with a tiny watercolour of a flower in one corner.

"Fucking 'ell,' Nina laughs, "You lot look as dodgy as ever. Where's Bob the Bastard, isn't this his van?"

Glazed eyes peer back out at us as Kenny, from somewhere deep in the pit of his brain, tries to smile and to work out who we are.

"Reeeeeehh .... d'you like m'new ketamine kit." he manages to dribble.

"I'm very impressed," says Nina. "What are you doing exactly?"

He holds up the bottle, looking very chuffed with himself.

"Liquid ketamine, innit, direct from India. Gotta cook it down to powder, 'fore we can stick it up our hooters, innit." Kenny manages to explain. "We're doing more 'cause some hairy cunt did my whole fucking wrap in."

Mad Bastard Bob grunts from the depths of his van, wrapped around a gas bottle, semi-conscious.

"Well... that's... ummm... nice, I guess," is all I can think to say, "Good that you came prepared."

"Dibdibdibdobdobdob, like a good boy scout," howls Nina, laughing at her own joke while shaking Kenny's head from side to side with one hand stretched across the top of his skull.

"Good kit, innit," says Kenny, slowly being reclaimed by the k-hole he was in. "Got it all from fag tokens, you know ... out of the Focus point catalogue. ... stove, saucepans ... the fucking lot ... came through yesterday ... just in time ..."

This sentence is punctuated by long, strained, outward breaths, accompanied by frantic gurning; the effort of concentrating and communicating is becoming too much. Me and Nina politely decline the big, lumpy line of K offered our way by one of the cave dwellers, and leave them to it. Even on a site full of grime, that is a particularly grimy corner.

We bimble on over towards Tash's big white van, checking corners for the shit-faced Bruce as we go. Next to the gate there is a battered old bath with a skinny little bloke folded into it, fast asleep, so cute that Nina practically climbs in for a cuddle.

Tash is sitting in the side doorway of her summer home, with her legs swinging backwards and forwards, looking like an Enid Blyton character after a re-write by Hunter S Thompson. The three of us have a group hug, then she motions into the back of the van with an exaggerated "ssshhhhhh". We look in and start giggling at the pile of sweaty, unconscious people on the bed at the back, six or seven sets of limbs cuddling up together, dreaming drugged-up dreams, pulling the blankets back and forth, and grumbling in their sleep. Nina laughs – Bruce is snuggled in, his arm draped around Dreads Dave. Somehow even they are managing to look cute, despite the hair and the dirt.

I'm still not sure I can skin up, so I pass Tash my suddenly quite small lump of pot and ask her to do the business. The three of us sit, talking about our night, our week, our lives. It's easy in the sunshine; all of us are dislocated from everyday reality, but we are close enough to each other to make it work. It's lovely.

Nina starts laughing.

"What the fuck is that," she says, pointing at Acid Bob and Goon. Bob looks like he normally does in the morning at a party – dusty jeans, dirty hands, bug-eyed sunglasses – but he is now topped off by an electric blue woolly bobble hat, which is pulled tight over his ears. The oversized pompom flops backwards and forwards as he lurches through the crowds, soaking up the appreciative laughter and over-the-top compliments.

"Where did that come from?" someone shouts, and he gestures behind him. Beyond Goon, who is looking very dashing in a natty straw boater, Foxie is stalking about with a black bin liner full of hats. He delves into the bag and hands one of those bright green sun visor things to Gollum who is laid on his back in the sunshine; the green light that filters onto his face makes him look even more alien than usual. Next out is a battered black top hat which is given to Gonzo dancing by the warehouse doors. It is *perfect* for his tall, skinny, clad-in-black body, Velvet Underground shades and wild, two foot long hair. Foxie beams a big smile, happy with his work, before heading into the warehouse.

"Where'd they all come from, where'd he get them from?" Tash shouts over to Bob.

"He did all the tat-shops on Gloucester Road, got loads of them, just for the crack," he replies, bobble wobbling around his head. I look at Tash. Tash looks at Nina. Nina looks at me. Words are unnecessary. We just sit in the sun swinging our legs, sharing a spliff, laughing with and at our very special friends.

Life is effortless. Life is sweet.

Back in the warehouse the music has picked up speed again for one last blast, and there is freaky dancing all around. The crowd is sparse but deeply wired into the tunes. Some sway around, moving in time with every eighth or sixteenth beat, some move nothing but their heads – double-time, about 300 beats per minute. When they next wake up they are going to have no idea why their neck hurts quite so badly. There is a glowing couple down by the speaker. I don't know if they were a couple when they came out tonight but they definitely are now. They're standing barely three inches apart, mirroring each other, quivering, arms moving just a fraction, and there's just the slightest half-time jerk of their hips. They don't blink. They just stare into each others eyes. They are *totally* locked in place, feeling what the other feels, delving deep into each other, all without actually touching. The anticipation is everything. They stand there fixated with each other for tune after tune after tune, oblivious to every other movement around them. They may as well be alone in the universe, just the two of them. They need no one and nothing else. Love is being constructed before our eyes.

I pop my head out of the warehouse, wondering what the crew are planning to do, while wanting to keep dancing until the last possible moment. Caspar has driven his car as close to the doors as he can and Rez and Little My are stomping up and down on it, caving the roof in beneath their big fuck-you boots.

"I'm dumping it tomorrow for the insurance, so fuck it!" he tells anyone who asks.

Nina has got Chumpee by the dreads and isn't letting go, sporadically slipping her arm through his, then dancing round him, twirling the four foot length of hair as she goes.

"Time to go?" he says to me and the surrounding group of broken, danced-out people. In the background a banger comes in, hard and heavy, fast and furious; an old hardcore classic reclaimed for dirty techno.

"Yeah," says Gonzo. "But one last dance, just this tune?"

"Fuck it, why not," is the collective reply, and we stomp back in en masse, twenty-five or so of us, whooping and hollering, giving it loads, doubling the number of dancers still on the floor. The weird stabbing, rising, bass-note that anchors the tune comes in and we go mad, hands in the air like its peak time two o'clock in the morning. The DJ grins a massive smile at us and bounces from foot to foot, punching the air with a record in his hand. I look around, proud of the crew that feels like family to me. Beautiful weird people, dancing with passion, dancing with feeling, dancing with meaning. The tune fades into comedy chart-techno, *I Wanna*

Be a Hippy, and we laugh and smile and as one twirl back towards the door, leaving the dancefloor looking depleted without us, clapping the crew behind the decks and the dancers still going for it. The pile of munters sat by the doors give us a round of applause as we stomp out. We applaud them back. Then we are out of the gates and onto the main road.

Back into the real world.

11 / Quench — Dreams

I have very little idea of how we get anywhere, but we do. There are long stretches of autopilot, where my body's entrenched systems just take over and keep me breathing, walking, blinking. Long stretches of nothing, just a blank where my consciousness should be. But we've definitely left, I'm sure of that. This isn't the party anymore.

It's not too bad to start with, just the odd car flying along the back roads that stretch from this abandoned part of town towards civilisation. We laugh and shout at each other, floating along on the rush of the night for a while. It's sunny – pure blue skies – and fucking hot. We realise just how far we are from our rough little home patch and begin to stagger rather than stride; a desiccated line of crusties and hippies and goths and students and indie-kids and punks and dreads and freaks, drawing stares as we pass pockets of normal humanity going about its business. The little liquid we have is quickly shared, and we try to plan a route that will take us past an open shop or a garage.

Thinking is hard.

And the roads seem to go on.

And on.

And on.

And on.

And on.

And on.

And on.

And on.

The city alienates us. Too fucked to drive, too mangled and skint to even consider taxis, we are forced to walk through a city designed for cars. We strip a little corner shop bare, like booze and fag crazed locusts; as we skirt the centre of town the occasional Sunday shopper walks past us, clutching their bags to their chests as if the zombie invasion has started and no one told them, imagining we are about to eat them and nick their shop-fresh Primark clothes. We stick to the back roads, and are cutting through a park when Ramona spots a boot abandoned by a bunch of bushes that edge a children's playground.

"Wonder who's that is?" she says, "looks like it should belong to one of us."

She's right; it's a big ostentatious leather thing, with extra straps, chunky black buckles, and hand-drawn UV lines running around the edge of the two inch thick platform sole. We wonder how much further some munter has walked before realising they have only got one shoe on.

"Isn't that Little Sam's boot?" mumbles Arthur, walking towards it.

A head pops out of the bushes – it's Little Sam, very flushed.

"Can't someone get a bit of privacy when they crawl into a fucking bush?" she grins.

"A fucking bush is it?" laughs McKay, "who you got in there with you for fucking then?"

A slurred voice comes from the undergrowth, "Jus' ignor'em Sam c'mere."

"Is that you Gollum, you dirty fucker?" shouts Caspar.

"Fukoffffff," comes the cheerful reply.

Sam's head disappears back into the scrub, and an arm stretches out from the bottom, grabs the boot and vanishes again.

"Dirty fuckers," shouts Rez.

"Won't somebody think of the children," wails Nina.
"Don't forget yer condoms kids," Little My joins in.
"Fuck *offfffffffff!*"

We are through the park and back onto the right side of town. It's not often that I am this happy to see the front door of St Nicks, the rented house that feels like a squat that I share with Chumpee, Gonzo and Zak, and that has also at various times been home to Little My, Mona, Gollum, and more. Right now it looks like a palace.

The house slowly fills with the bedraggled convoy of munters, who are soon dancing in every corner, draped over every chair, and slumped like piles of old rags on the floor. Gonzo hands out beers; Polly tries to get a round of teas together. I stick some tunes on and Helen runs to the shop to buy a loaf of cheap white bread and some butter. The smell of toast soon drifts through the house. It's bloody lovely. Perfect with a cup of tea.

Chumpee gets straight to work, taking an old vodka bottle and smashing the bottom off of it by putting two heavy handled knives inside, spinning the bottle round and round, then giving a swift up-and-down jerk. The bottom comes off clean, the edge sharp but not jagged. He sets out about twenty fingertip-sized lumps of weed on a plate and the ends of the knives go into the flame of the hob until red-hot; the weed is then dabbed and burnt into the bottle between the two ends in one smooth movement. A queue forms, stretching into the hall, everyone taking it in turns to inhale through the bottletop. When I get to the front of the queue I do Chumpee's first, as he has already done about ten people by then, picking one of the biggest bits for him. In return he picks a particularly large lump for me, which completely kicks my head in. I walk back down the hall towards the front room, only upright because my skull scrapes along the wall all the way, bumping over the light switch and clattering past the doorframe. I make it to a sofa and sink deep in, surrounded by people and dogs, warm and fuzzy. The music's blaring, a classic Billy Nasty tape thumping away, and people are fucking having it in the corners of the room, unable to stop. Lines go round, but I know I'm at my limits for a minute.

Nat appears, having swung by her house to get the beer bong – a five foot length of tube, with a funnel on one end and a little tap at the bottom. Before long she has a parallel production line to Chumpee, with people kneeling at her feet, pouring their drink of choice in through the top. The tap is then opened and gravity does the rest, bomph, straight down your gullet, pissed as fuck within minutes. Huge vodka drinks, whole cans of lager and half bottles of cider disappear in split-seconds. From the looks of it, it kicks your head in just as successfully as the hot-knives. I wouldn't know, as there is no way in the world I am touching that right now.

I think I sleep for a few minutes at some point, because the next thing I know everyone is getting ready to go to the pub. Gonzo descends the stairs from his room, immaculate in a clean black t-shirt, hair scraped back into a monstrous ponytail, shades clamped to his face, looking utterly together.

"Feeling fresh?" McKay asks him, thinking he's just got up.

Gonzo gives him a beautiful grin in return, as if a thoughtful answer is on its way.

"Blah, blah, blah," is all that comes out.

He decides to repeat it.

"Blah, blah blah."

He smiles again, adjusts his shades, and then marches down the hall towards the front door. How he can walk so

purposefully when he can't even talk is beyond me. McKay is in stitches at the bottom of the stairs.

The pub isn't far, maybe a twenty-minute lurch through the quiet Sunday afternoon inner-city streets. Most of the local bad boys are still tucked up in bed; we only get offered rocks twice. The attention we do get is mainly because Little My has decided to wear Chumpee's dressing gown to the pub and it's not immediately evident what else she's got on underneath. Through a graffiti covered railway tunnel, and into a dead-end surrounded by a city farm and allotments, a few terraced houses, and a yard full of traveller wagons, we make it without getting pulled by the police or losing too many of our crew to random distractions.

The pub itself sits at the end of a big sloping garden, and it's fucking packed. Every patch of grass, every bench, every old stable is covered in shit-faced munters. Half the party crew from last night are sprawled in the dotted afternoon sun, the other half are inside dancing like loons to the DJ in the corner. The beats drift over the chatter and everyone bobs along. There's a line-factory in operation in the stables, mind your head on the way in, snort something, then stagger back out into the world, slightly more wrong than a second before.

Nina and the rest of the bar staff, and the landlords, were all at the warehouse last night, so they know the score; they're just as fucked as the rest of us, more so probably. It's so fucking busy inside – crammed full of people squeezed up against each other with barely room to breathe. An old-school house tune drops – big vocals and everything – and I think the building is going to burst as people jump and shout. The adventure playground next door is full as well; kids having a laugh, their parent's peering over the fence from the pub garden every now and again.

It may be nearly 5 o'clock on a Sunday afternoon, but really it's still just a Saturday night out. It's warm, with a lovely breeze drifting through. Time blurs into hellos and laughs and stories and questions and not many answers. Wondering where some people are, marvelling at some peoples ability to keep going. Occasionally I zone out, away from the shouting and raucousness around me, and I'm conscious of the planes passing overhead, of children laughing in the background, of the wind pushing through the tops of the trees.

Normal life carries on out there, carries on without us. That's fine.

People draw on each others faces, rough and tumble across the grass, hang out of the upstairs windows having shouted conversations with those down below. Rez and Esther start dancing on our table and at the far end of the garden a couple of blokes try to do the same thing, but bump each other, making both of them fall. Everyone laughs.

At some point I lay my head on a table, my hand still gripped round a shot of whiskey, intending to psyche myself up to down it. Instead there is darkness.

I'm walking again, arm in arm with someone. Two someone's. One on each side. Up a hill. Why am I walking up a hill?

"Why am I walking up a hill?" I ask.

"On our way to Grace's house," says Rez, on one side.

"Oh, thanks," I say, happy to know I'm being looked after, "which one?" I ask Little My, on my other arm.

"Not sure," she laughs, "I only met them last night.

Up ahead I can see a line of people, including a good proportion of the original crew that stepped out together yesterday. That's good endurance, right there. Who says the youth of today have no stamina? Just in front of us

Chumpee and Nina walk arm-in-arm; she sporadically tries to make him give her a piggyback, running around him and launching herself onto him, nearly knocking him over.

"He's pulled then," laughs Rez.

There's another front room. More drugs are taken at various points. A line of MDMA that makes everything glow and slow down. A cheeky little quarter here and there. Bubbly tunes drift around the room and people rub each others' backs. The atmosphere thickens and coalesces around us, all of us feeling very comfortable in each others personal space. Grace rubs my shoulders, and when she runs the tips of her fingers up my spine and neck and then pulls away from my crown I feel that golden thread of light sweep up through me again, bursting out of the top of my head, chasing the glowing ends of her fingertips. The next time I walk I am Mr Soft, unable to fully straighten my legs, mooching through the streets, surrounded by similarly loose-limbed fabulous furry freaks.

We head to a huge local park to watch the sun go down. The sunset is beautiful, drifting down over the distant hills. The sky changes colour every second and the spring growth on the trees changes with it, reflecting its glory. Darkness spreads from behind us, individual stars popping into sight.

We are awestruck.

Another pub. Later now. I don't seem to have anything at all in my pockets anymore, but I have a drink in front of me and a spliff in my hand, so I'm alright. My house key is still on a string around my neck, cold against my sternum. I'm upstairs in the pool room at our local, in a room that operates outside normal licensing laws. The shelves in the toilets are grooved from years of line-chopping, skinning-up is standard, and last orders is viewed as an interesting theory. There are loads of us here still vaguely awake. And one or two asleep on a bench. Have I been asleep?

"Have I been asleep?" I ask the person sat next to me. It's Zak.

"No, but you have been very quiet for a while. Maybe you were asleep but you forgot to shut your eyes."

I look at the pool tables – from the chalkboard I can see it's the Sunday night pool competition, and that somehow Gonzo has made it to the final. The tracers from the balls flash around as he plays and pots every single one, seven-balling his challenger straight from the break.

"Blah, blah, blah," he says with a smile, shaking their hand before swaggering down to the bar to collect his liquid winnings, like a big goth cowboy.

I spark the spliff and hand it to Zak, both of us laughing at the stunned face of his opponent.

Someone's garden? On a hill somewhere? Doesn't really matter – there are people everywhere. Dark again, but not cold. Half the pub still on a roll, more happy faces from last night who have reappeared from somewhere. I wonder what adventures they have had today. Drink is flowing, hash smoke is rising, beats are gently bumping. Faces glow in the light of the bonfire.

I lie back onto the soft grass, feeling the midnight dew on the back of my neck, and stare into the stars.

So many stars.

12 / The Ecstasy Boys – Seven Steps to Heaven

The regular flash of streetlights makes my eyelids shine silver-red when seen from the inside, my brain conscious for a few seconds before my body catches up and drags the thin skin from over my eyes. The streets are deserted. We drive down an inner-city dual carriageway, past the offices of the local paper. The huge red lettering of the third storey dot matrix sign says "03:30 15 MAY 1995".

Fuck, it's only two days 'til my birthday. Twenty-one on Wednesday. Fucking hell. Twenty-one.

The car carries me through time and space, my head disembodied, separate from the rest of my fragile flesh, battered beyond belief. Aching from dancing, numb from exhaustion, tingling from whatever drugs I took last; my cheeks are aching from laughing and smiling and smiling and laughing. I glance at the driver, wondering whose hands my life is in. Not someone I recognise, but that's Chumpee's laugh I can hear coming from the passenger seat in front of me.

"Where we heading geezer?" I croak.

"Up to Hog's, to get some supplies. You alright?"

"Could murder a cup of tea…"

"Won't be long – this is Henry by the way, mate from Manchester, he got down just as the pub was shutting, so I thought he might as well drive us. Hehehehe, I'm too fucked to walk anywhere…"

"Hello Henry," I mumble.

"'Alright, mate," he says, "Comfy enough for yer, back there?"

"Yes thanks."

They burble on, catching up. I watch the world fly by, amazed at how normal it all still looks.

Home again. Less people now. Curtains closed defiantly against the rising sun. An unwelcome intruder. Bottles and cans litter the floor, the ashtrays are full. Washed-out people lie around the place, watching some comedy, the weirder the better. Laughing feels brilliant.

I can hear McKay in the hall on the phone, half a laugh escaping from his throat, because Chumpee's dancing like a gibbon up and down the hall, trying to put him off. The video clock says 8:37am.

"Fuck offfff," McKay whispers.

Then into the phone, "Oh, hello there. It's Charlie McKay here. I'm *awfully* sorry but I can't come into work today, as I have a cold. Sniff."

He does a half-hearted cough.

Chumpee is still monkey-dancing, when a pen dings off his forehead. I can hear the phone cable flapping about as McKay does a little victory jig.

"Uh, what... sorry... ok, yes, sorry, awfully sorry, yes, I will be in tomorrow," he slurs into the phone, losing his concentration, now just enjoying chucking stuff at Chumpee – pencils, paperclips, pages ripped out of the phonebook. As he hangs up we all parrot "I'm awfullllllly sorry" from the front room, pissing ourselves laughing. I say a silent thank you that I don't have to do anything until Wednesday. Mustn't forget to sign on.

I go to put the kettle on.

"Stick the knives on again," Chumpee shouts as I stagger down the hall.

The video we are watching stops; I yawn and stretch and look around the room. Chumpee is half asleep in the big chair, with Nina curled up on his lap. Gonzo and Fran are on the little sofa, Zak, Dreads Dave and Jasper, half-sat, half-slumped on the floor in front. Jasper's been skinning up for about forty-five minutes. So far he has got two skins together. The wrong way round. Gollum is asleep on the long sofa, scrunched up against Donna, Ray, and Grace. A pile of unidentifiable people are asleep in the corner. The sunlight seeps through the edges of the curtains, but dissipates into the thick fug of smoke that hangs in the room, losing the courage of its convictions and drifting to a halt halfway in. I can hear other voices laughing from the kitchen – Goon, Caspar, Rez, others – and music and dancing in the back room.

"Right that's me done," I say, dragging my sorry carcass from the little chair I've been curled in.

"I'm done, that's it, got to go to bed. Night all."

Semi-conscious hugs are exchanged, commemorating the end of a fantastic weekend. What a fucking laugh. I love the people in that room with a depth of feeling I didn't know existed. For all kinds of reasons – for sharing that experience, for understanding how good I felt, for moving with and around me, for making it the night that it was – they feel like family.

It feels good.

The clock in the kitchen says it's half two. It's Monday afternoon. I stagger up the stairs, land on the mattress and zone out for a moment. There's a body in the bed already, snoring away.

I realise I am tapping my feet to an imaginary beat that is thumping through my head, a mix of rhythmic tinnitus and the pounding of my heart. I should put some music on. I zone out again.

Moving quickly is a mistake – I sit up, spin out and lie back down again. My mind swirls around my skull, sloshing about all over the place. I must have music. The silence is too loud. All I can hear is the blood roaring through the capillaries of my brain, sending my thoughts spinning and whirling along with it.

I need to float.

Slowly this time, keeping my head low, I crawl to the stereo and select some spacey beats. I lie back down with a satisfying sound in my ears; my boots slip off my feet and I slump onto the covers.

The whole weekend feels like a dream, like something just out of reach, just over the horizon.

Was it real?

Did it really happen?

Were they real feelings?

The thought spirals around my head for a moment before I get a grip and laugh at it.

Of course it was real.

Those moments, those movements, those sounds, those feelings – they all really happened.

The afterglow from sharing those experiences with thousands of people – with hundreds of thousands of people over the years – can keep you warm for a long time, if you let it.

The music seeps into my brain and I forget about undressing. I sense the warm body next to me and, still smiling, fall asleep. We dream together. We dream of the past and we dream of a future.

We hear music.

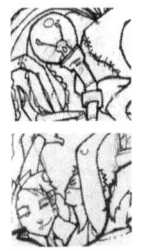

SILENT HOBO
01/02/04/05/07/08/12

Silent Hobo is a traditionalist, sticking to the can rather than stencils. A character-based artist whose style is a mix of comic art influenced by early graffiti, manga and 2000AD. His characters can be seen around Bristol on walls, in community centres, pubs, libraries, train stations, and at festivals. In the studio Silent Hobo concentrates on making artwork, which he sells as limited edition prints. His pictures mix photography with illustration to create stylised and beautifully composed scenes.

www.silenthobo.co.uk

NIK ILL
03/06

Nik Ill is an artist from Bristol with a fine flowing line and a sharp eye for detail. Following well-received work on walls and canvas, as well as a successful range of t-shirts, he is now studying 'Motion Graphics and Visual Effects' at London Metropolitan University, in-between smashing dancefloors with his new band, 'The Hit-Ups'.

www.myspace.com/lovetheleaf

BOSWELL
09

Boswell (aka Warp) has been creating art for as long as he can remember, often working with fellow crew members from the progressive graffiti group - SOF - which he helped to create. His influences transcend the generic Graffiti themes. Mediaeval art, gothic literature and film, sci-fi, and comics are some of the reference points. His work has a unique edge; half-beast, half-human characters inhabit an unstable world of elemental forces and lost technologies, mutating to create a universe of new possibilities.

www.boswellart.co.uk

ROSE SANDERSON
10

Rose has lived in Bristol for 11 years and is based at the renowned Jamaica Street Artists Studios. Her art is influenced by natural history, anatomy, insects, and strange creatures. Where others may see disgust or distaste, Rose sees beauty and intrigue.

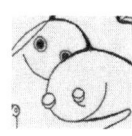

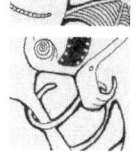

www.rosesanderson.com

NATALIE SANDELLS
11

Natalie Sandells is a freelance illustrator and comic artist living in London in the UK. She primarily does concept art, illustrations, and comic work for the gaming and graphic novel industries, though in the past she has been approached for work in TV and film. She works in a variety of mediums, ranging from brush & ink to digital techniques.

www.natsan.com

MATTHEW SMITH
Inside covers

For over two decades Matthew Smith (aka Mattko) has been making his distinctive brand of social documentary, reportage, and portraiture. His work is part-diary, part-document, part citizen photojournalism, and looks at music, protest, art and culture. His work is an astounding collection of images, rooted in the people who have given us some of the most wonderful movements, music and memories of the last twenty years.

www.mattko.tumblr.com

A

01: Joey Beltram – Energy Flash (Transmat Records)
02: Jones & Stevenson – The First Rebirth (Prolekult Records)
03: Robotman – Do-Da-Doo (Plastikman Acid House Mix) (Definitive Recordings)
04: Tim Taylor & Dan Zamani – Planet of Drums ! (Planet of Drums Records)
05: Emmanuel Top – Tone (Attack Records)
06: Hardfloor – Aceperience (Harthouse Records)
07: DJ Misjah & Tim – Access (X-Trax Records)
08: Union Jack – Cactus (Platypus Records)
09: Pump Panel – Ego Acid (Missile Records)
10: Nexus-6 – Tres-Chic (Woom Records)
11: Hard Trance – Extraordinary (Scott Brown Mix) (Evolution Records)

12: Green Nuns of the Revolution – Cor (TIP Records)
13: The Infinity Project – Feeling Weird (TIP Records)
14: Unknown – "Bulbous" (Unknown)
15: DJ Misjah – X-Pact (X-Trax Records)
16: Wippenberg – Neurodancer (Prolekult Records)
17: Acrid Abeyance – Speed Freak (Important Rec...)
18: Dr. Octopus – Dr. Octopus (Millennium Records)

SPANNERED !

⊗TDK

SPANNERED 2

19: Starpower – Renegade 303 (Stay Up Forever Records)
20: Josh Wink – Higher State of Consciousness (Tweeking Acid Funk Mix) (Strictly Rhythm)
21: Orbital – Chime (ffrr)
22: CJ Bolland – The Prophet (R & S Records)
23: Gambol 202 – Blue Index (23 Frankfurt)
24: Jonny L – The Ansaphone (XL Recordings)
25: New Order – Confusion (Pump Panel Reconstruction) (Factory Records)
26: 4D – Hidden (Labworks Germany)
27: Ed Rush, Optical and Fierce – Cutslo (Locust Mix) (Prototype Recordings)
28: Damon Wild & Tim Taylor – Bang The Acid (Sinewave)
29: Technohead – The Passion (Mokum Records)
30: Jon the Dentist – Destiny (Arena of the Gods Mix) (Boscaland Records)
31: Technohead – I Wanna Be A Hippy (Mokum Records)
32: Quench – Dreams (Infectious Records)
33: Vinyl Blair – Housework (Vinyl's Source Radish Mix) (Music Man Records)
34: Alison Limerick – Where Love Lives (Arista Records)
35: Leftfield – Release The Pressure (Hard Hands)
36: The Ecstasy Boys – Seven Steps to Heaven (Quark Records)
37: Orbital – Belfast (ffrr)